PIECES

⋮

PIECES

Afshan Malik

⋮

rabata
Daybreak Press

Pieces by Afshan Malik was first published 2019 by:

Daybreak Press | 3533 Lexington Avenue | Arden Hills, MN 55126 | USA

Online: rabata.org/daybreakpress | Email: daybreakpress@rabata.org

© 2019 by Daybreak Press, reprinted in 2023 with corrections

All Rights Reserved

Pieces is a work of fiction; names, characters, places, and incidents are the product of the author's imagination and are used fictitiously and are not to be construed as real. Any resemblance to actual events, organizations, locales, or persons, living or dead, is entirely coincidental.

Library of Congress Control Number: 2018968248
ISBN: 978-0-9992990-1-2

Cover art: Nancy French, *Lindenlea Paper, Ottawa, ON, Canada*: lindenleapaper.ca
Cover design: Reyhana Ismail, *Rey of Light Design*: reyoflightdesign.com
Interior design and typesetting: scholarlytype.com

Printed in the United States of America

This book is dedicated to to my husband. Thank you for your unconditional faith, when you know what I'm up to and when you don't.

⋮

1

Clouds wove patterns in the sky. Hannah rested her head against the back of a wrought iron bench and let herself become distracted from the people weaving in and out of the entrance to Winthrop Medical Center. The breeze was balmy and soothing. The clouds weren't heavy or dense with rain yet, but it wouldn't take long for storm clouds to roll in and toss a wet blanket over their little southern town. Her jeans rolled over her well-worn sneakers, and the frayed edges touched the floor. The fingers of one hand played with the charms of the bracelet on her other hand. In the clouds, she spotted a ship, a baby carriage, and what seemed to be a vague shape of wings that, had she had the opportunity to think further, would resemble an angel with its wings curved forward as if to offer warmth and hope. Her musings were interrupted by a car alarm going off in the parking lot. The sky was Hannah's favorite thing to sketch when she wasn't busy. It wasn't confined or structured.

The circular driveway that graced the hospital's front entrance was constantly bustling. New mothers, the sick trying to make it from their wheelchairs into waiting cars, and those who must have been freshly released from the ER, with casts and crutches, emerged from the hospital, making their way past visitors with balloons and plants headed in the opposite direction.

The automatic doors swooshed open. Out of the corner of her eye, Hannah caught a glimpse of her older sister's bright yellow messenger bag and swiveled her body toward her. She watched her sister, followed by her mom, get closer; their pace steady, their faces composed. Her sister Noreen's face was aloof and unconcerned. Hannah supposed she practiced in front of the mirror. Noreen was shorter than Hannah, but a few years older. Hannah had shot up over the past two years, whereas Noreen, at a delicate five feet even, exuded an aura of being dainty and non-threatening.

Hannah's mom's face radiated calmness, and Hannah knew she barely looked in the mirror. Her routine had become so stream-lined over the years that Hannah could mimic the exact way she would roll her hair in a bun at the base of her neck every morning before going to work. The style in which she wore her scarf never changed, nor did the location where she hooked in a straight pin to keep it all in place. Noreen took after her in looks and height. They both stood at a five feet even, with eyes that anchored to the object of their attention.

"Ready to go, sweetie?" Dahlia asked. She held the keys to their old, black suburban. The key-chain was hooked to her finger.

Hannah came with her mom and sister every weekend to the hospital. She spent most of the few hours reading or people watching. After a traumatic first visit, she'd refused to go inside again.

Hannah half nodded, indicating she was prepared to leave. She stood up, towering above her sister and mother by an entire five inches. She stretched her neck side to side in a slow roll and reached her arms towards the sky. Her body was sore from track practice the afternoon before, and her muscles silently moaned with the slow movements. The junior high coach had brought in a new whistle to motivate the team to move faster in their sprinting drills. The shrill pitch succeeded in annoying them enough to spur them on.

"How was he today?" Hannah asked.

"Sleepy, but stable. Dr. Finland was in earlier today and I missed him by a few minutes, but the nurses updated me on the changes in medication," her mom explained, taking a deep breath of the pleasant air. Dr. Finland was head of the psychiatric department at the hospital, and Dahlia knew him well because his office was in the same adjacent medical building as her own practice.

"I also ran into Dr. Pope." Hannah's mother referenced her colleague. "He and I may be collaborating on a new seminar with expectant mothers and homeopathic techniques to ease the stress of labor." She continued to chatter about her plans.

Hannah tuned her out, as she normally did when her mother got to explaining different theories in ob-gyn. The hospital staffed her as a physician and also as a consultant to lead different programs for students going into medicine at the nearby university. She finished up her explanation with an air of expectancy, so Hannah nodded and murmured sounds of interest and approval.

Both looked at Noreen for her take.

Noreen was thumbing away at her cell phone and had already reached the edge of the elaborate awning. Her fingers effortlessly played the keypad on the smartphone screen, and the phone buzzed while she was still texting - one alert, then two, then three.

Dahlia eyed the phone and then her. She cleared her throat dramatically. Noreen looked up, made eye contact, and sighed. The phone disappeared.

Noreen had been subject to a few long talks about using her cell phone with such consistency. Dahlia was close to banning it when they were all together. It had started out as an emergency phone after Noreen had started driving to school and spiraled into something that never left her side. According to Noreen, everyone she knew had owned a cell phone since junior high, and since she hadn't been allowed one until it had seemed logical to their parents, she seemed to be making up for lost time.

Their mother nodded at her with thanks. She then turned to Hannah, whose hands were in her sweatshirt pockets, gazing blankly in the distance. "You know you're welcome to come in any time you'd like, Hannah," she said.

Noreen rolled her eyes. "I think it's been weeks since she's graced the halls with her presence. God forbid we step out of our comfort zone," she scoffed. Noreen's feelings on Hannah's unwavering resolve not to return to the hospital itched under her skin intensely. She thought her younger sister was selfish. Selfish and avoiding reality.

Dahlia hooked her arm into Hannah's and squeezed. Her mouth curved into a comforting smile as she looked up at her younger daughter's withdrawn face. "Don't mind Noreen," she said, an undertone of apology slipping into her voice. "She almost panicked when she thought the hand sanitizer was empty at the nurse's station. And when we were just about finished with our visit, a nurse roped her into taking some children's books to the second floor and organizing them. She was actually pretty gracious about it," commended their mother, arching her eyebrow to share the surprise with Hannah.

"Let's try to keep that graciousness going, even among ourselves," her mother finished with a nod, holding Noreen's gaze.

These days, to Hannah, Noreen being gracious was about as easy to imagine as an elephant threading a needle.

As they left the parking lot, they nodded hello to various visitors. Small towns were friendly. Both Noreen and Hannah had been born in Dallas, but they had moved further south, near Houston, when the girls were in grade school. Still an hour from downtown, they got to enjoy the perks of being far enough away from the hustle and bustle of a city to enjoy some serenity. The South in general was courteous; there was an ingrained sense of hospitality and good manners. Strangers helped strangers and neighbors took their duties seriously.

People who saw you often at the hospital felt close enough to ask how you were doing, what you were headed in for, and who it was that took up few hours of your Saturday each week to visit. Everyone who was a regular became a part of that familiarity. Familiarity isn't really a good thing when it comes to hospitals, though. Frequent visits mean a problem that isn't being solved. But at least that familiarity comforted you that you weren't alone in the surreal twilight zone between sickness and health.

As small as that comfort was, it was there.

An older man tipped his hat at their trio as he parked his truck and started around it to help his wife out. She was frail, with wispy hair and a wispier voice. He unloaded her wheelchair to unfold it, then lifted her out of the passenger seat. Hannah had seen them several times before. Her outpatient appointments were through the same entrance, but down another hall. That hall was filled with local artists' work depicting bright gardens and harmonious nature scenes.

Marigolds. Orchids. Sunflowers. Tulips. Luscious trees with bright green, crisp leaves. Hannah knew them well. She would sometimes walk through the main floor hallways when it was too humid to wait outside.

Weeping willows didn't make the cut, she recalled. Weeping willows might feel a touch depressing. Hannah remembered overhearing conversations about which paintings would grace the walls on one of her rambles.

Winthrop Medical was a research-run medical institution. Hannah's mother often held classes or seminars in their state-of-the-art auditorium, when she wasn't seeing patients at her private practice or delivering babies at the hospital. For a small town hospital, it was always busy and had a steady stream of visitors and medical professionals walking briskly through its corridors. Sometimes the hospital held community programs for families who had loved ones in the hospital long term. It was a cross between a support group meeting and an awkwardly forced friendship. Hannah attended once. The refreshments tasted too sugary and the room felt small.

Windows would help, Hannah thought. A room full of windows.

During that meeting, the director of outpatient and rehabilitation programs had welcomed everyone. She was short, round, and wore horn-rimmed glasses that weren't flattering, but definitely reflected her spunky personality. The information session jargon included phrases like *"Your loved ones will be loved...at the height of research and service...top-notch care...."*

Sure thing.

Hannah, with her mother and sister, hopped into their car as the wind picked up. It had shifted from balmy to breezy. Once they were on the road headed back home, tree branches waved against a backdrop of graying skies. The rain started. One drop, then several, splattered against their windshield. It was comforting rather than dreary. A good downpour was something they could enjoy together.

Everyone in her family enjoyed the rain. There were afternoons it would rain and everyone would gather at the wide bay windows in the den. Their backyard held several stately old trees, and the patterned sheets of rain were a magical sight as they fell from dozens of tree branches.

The silence lasted until they reached a shop just a few blocks from home. Five years ago, new owners had taken over and instead of limiting it to baked goods and delicacies, they had added the much-needed flair of fancy coffees and seasonal drinks. Hannah's mother stopped at the stoplight and, with a deliberately light voice, said, "How about we grab some pastries and make hot chocolate at home? I'm sure you two could use a treat after the past few weeks of midterms and projects. I've been buried in paperwork for days because of some new insurance policy changes. I definitely need a treat for surviving that."

Noreen agreed and volunteered to go in as Dahlia pulled into the parking lot and parked the car.

"Can I get whatever I want?" she asked, unbuckling herself from the seat and reaching for the door handle.

Dahlia paused, then consented, laughing. "I had to do a quick mental check to make sure there wasn't anything too healthy in the bakery. Go ahead. Surprise us."

"Cool," Noreen said as leaped out the door and dashed the 10 feet into the coffee shop. Once she was in, even the neon yellow of her messenger bag disappeared from sight, despite the brightly lit interior and floor to ceiling windows. Sometimes she would get into super healthy moods and would wreak havoc, making sure things were gluten, dairy, soy, and whatever else was fashionable at the moment to avoid-free.

Hannah remained silent in the backseat. She would often walk to this bakery and eat mini truffles with her friend, Ashley. Ashley's parents rarely let her out of the house to hang with friends, but since this was within view of their home, they consented.

The library was another few blocks down the street, so the girls would make excursions there on lazy weekends. For the past several weeks, however, Hannah's weekends had been completely booked. Track practice on Fridays after school and hospital visits on Saturdays. She still considered her trip a visit, even if she didn't go inside. Sundays were saved for catching up on home-work and furiously rubbing a lint roller over her clothes because their old cat Zuzu seemed to find Hannah's clothes - folded, unfolded, laundered, or dirty - the best to lounge on when no one was home.

As they waited for Noreen to finish her purchase, the rain-drops fell rhythmically and lulled both mother and daughter into silence. After a few minutes, Dahlia spoke.

"You haven't said much today," she made her voice chipper. "How are you doing these days? Was the past week overwhelming because of your exams? Did track practice go well? Mary Anne's mother texted saying her ears were ringing by the time you girls were done. Something about a new whistle?"

Hannah shifted as her mother questioned her. As gently as she had done it, her questioning was still hanging in the air, forcing Hannah to respond. She sighed. Usually she wouldn't have minded a conversation with her mom. It was Noreen who avoided mom talks. And even she could hold basic conversations that were civil, if not necessarily pleasant. But Hannah wasn't feeling much like sharing at the moment.

"It was okay," she finally mumbled. Inside her head, she pressured Noreen to hurry up so they could go home. At home she could at least hide in a book or make excuses about homework.

"Okay is nice," acknowledged Dahlia. "Okay is something we can work with." She paused slightly, her lips pursing, trying to battle with something in her mind. Hannah knew her mother's instinct was to push and press and prod her out of her quietude. But Hannah was naturally introverted, and her mother made it a point to acknowledge that and respect her quietness as she grew older. Dahlia's lips pursed for a moment and, after a few more seconds of the rain-filled silence, she spoke. "We missed you inside the hospital today. I know the last several times you didn't want to go in either." She hurried to add, "Which is perfectly fine - no one is pressuring you. I do think it may be something for you to think about for the future, though. Maybe give next weekend a try."

"Yeah," sighed Hannah. The pressure at the back of her neck created a nagging feeling. The first time she visited her father at the hospital, he'd been hooked up to wires and slept more than he was awake. Once he was alert enough to recognize his family, he zeroed in on Hannah and began to shout. He almost ripped the IV from where it was taped onto his wrist in an attempt to get out of bed. His voice was dry and cracked, the look in his eyes frantic and mad. She was terrified at the changes in him. He was bruised and hysterical. Nurses were called in while her mother and Noreen tried to hold him down. Hannah froze in fright, afterwards refusing to return to his hospital room.

"I'll think about it," she finally agreed. Her fingers fiddled with the charms on her bracelet. One was a unicorn's head. The next a rose. An ice cream cone, the letter H, and a heart accompanied them. "Some of my friends were asking how he was doing, too."

The door popped open suddenly, and Noreen jumped inside the car. Her hoodie was spotted with raindrops. She removed the hood to reveal a gray and silver scarf, still pristine and dry, complimenting her creamy skin.

Two paper bags with a vibrant logo rustled by her feet on the passenger side. "I picked out something filled with chocolate, something with chocolate and nuts, and something else with chocolate and fruit." Noreen wooshed into the car, divulging the contents of her purchases, satisfied with her choices for their rainy afternoon treats.

Dahlia chimed in, "Sounds great! I'm going to find a recipe for some killer hot chocolate. It may get a little overpowering with all the additional chocolate, but I'm sure we can manage. We're tough like that. A rainy Saturday afternoon is the perfect excuse to indulge with my girls." Her tone switched from perky-fun to perky-business. "Hannah's friends have been asking about your dad, too. She's thinking about going back in to visit. *Inside*," she emphasized at the end. "Wouldn't that be nice?" she asked, half sounding hopeful and half declaring a breakthrough moment.

Noreen's eyes widened. Her slight frame twisted around to look at Hannah seated behind her. The blue of their mother's eyes had skipped Noreen, who wound up with glowing amber instead. They narrowed as she said, "So she told you?" She turned back around before seeing Hannah's mouth gape. "I figured she wouldn't want to, since she begged me for almost an hour not to say anything." It was usually Noreen that had to beg Hannah for silence when she stumbled upon something their mother wouldn't agree with. Hannah usually rolled her eyes at her sister's dramatic requests. Most of it was just self-created, since their mother was more likely to talk things to death in an attempt to compromise and reach an agreement than to lay down and enforce hard and fast rules.

"Told me what?" her mother quickly asked. Her face shifted to Noreen's quickly, then back to the road. "What is it? I knew there was something different."

The wipers moved in a monotonous motion, back and forth. They were sweeping streams of rain onto one side and the remnants were discarded at the bottom. Hannah imagined that her dilemma was somewhere in the massive amounts of rain that were being tossed every which way. Noreen had unceremoniously brought up a tidbit that had tilted the wipers of their mother's awareness toward her. And she was not one to let it go as easily as rain falling off the windshield.

Hannah stifled a growl of annoyance and exasperation. Her shoulders had stiffened and her eyes, which had sharpened with outrage, were burning a hole into the back of Noreen's seat.

"Noreen," their mother started with seriousness. "Hannah. I am going to be very polite and ask you girls what exactly is going on. I'm going to suggest you let me know now instead of five hours from now when all our tempers have been strained and there's no guarantee of my patience." She took a deep breath, Hannah observed, apparently bracing herself for the explanation. Maybe she thought Hannah had failed an exam. Got caught cheating or had performance issues on the field.

Mother bear claws were always at the ready when it came to their mom. First to rattle her kids and then to stride into battle with whomever may need to be dealt with.

Dahliah thought back to the morning, which had started quietly. Noreen wasn't exactly an early riser, so Hannah and her mother had had a quick breakfast together before starting on their own tasks. Hannah settled into the den and sprawled over the generously cushioned love seat with some books while her mother dictated patient notes. On a normal Saturday morning, Hannah would try out something in the kitchen or fiddle around with a DIY project like making candle holders out of mason jars. With glitter.

Lots of glitter.

The lack of glitter and contained chaos had tipped Dahliah off enough for her to ask if Hannah was feeling okay, but it wasn't until Hannah remained completely silent during their ride to the hospital and back that concern had really risen its worrisome head. Hannah knew it wasn't often her mother felt like she and Noreen unified against her to hide something.

When she did get a hint of it though, there was no place to hide.

"Ladies," she said in an even tone. It was smooth for now, but the next step was to lace it with a chilling undertone of icy politeness. The more she pressed for information or grew agitated, the more firm and rigid her speech became.

"Okay," Noreen said, starting to respond. She quickly glanced back at Hannah and then at their mother. As the car rolled into the driveway and stopped, they heard thunder rumble in the distance. One deep breath later, she jumped into the explanation. "Last night I was checking my email and Hannah's account was still logged on. She had a chat box open and one of her friends or whatever had messaged her. The message was asking her if she was doing okay and why she didn't let anyone know her dad had died."

Their mother's hands gripped the steering wheel, knuckles turning white. She stared outside the front windows, silent, not even drawing a breath. Her jaw slackened in disbelief for an instant, then clenched. She moved her head slightly to one side, then the other. It was as if the information was still trying to penetrate her mind. Unconsciously, she was moving her head faster to make the words seep in with more clarity.

Hannah sat still. She held her breath and watched her mother closely, afraid of her reaction. Noreen pressed her lips together and quickly moved her gaze from her mother to outside the passenger window. The bags of pastries didn't rustle now.

"Hannah Marlene Jamal," her mother choked out. She took a deep breath, and repeated: "Hannah. Marlene. Jamal." Each letter was enunciated carefully. The names carried a weight of their own. The weight seemed to roll into a muffling buzz in Hannah's ears. She was named Hannah after her great-aunt, whom Dahlia had grown close to on a trip to Spain. Marlene was for her mother's friend, who helped deliver her during a really bad storm when the roads were flooded and an ambulance couldn't make it in time. She was a sweet lady, a few years older than her mother, and a pediatrician by profession. She often wrote to the girls and visited Dahlia once every few years when she came to town for medical conferences.

"I cannot for the life of me comprehend what possessed you to imply to *anyone* that your father was *dead!*" After saying the word dead, her breath hitched. Her hands shifted from clutching the wheel to splaying themselves, fingers wide, in the air. "You may have your own insecurities about the situation our family is in, but I did not raise a liar and I do not intend to raise someone who wants to hide out from the truth by masking it under something so...so..." She stopped, at a loss for words.

Hannah's ears roared with embarrassment, humiliation, and guilt. "I didn't mean to," she sputtered quickly. "It was a conversation that got away from me and before I knew it someone thought he died and I didn't have a chance to correct them." Her guilt released in jerky movements as she edged closer to the end of her seat and held onto her sister's headrest, appealing to her mother's livid tone and stony face. "Noreen saw it and I asked her not to say anything. I felt bad for not visiting him all these weeks." She took a deep breath to rephrase. "I mean, I felt bad for not visiting anyway, but I felt bad about what happened yesterday, too, and…"

"Enough," her mother whispered. "We can continue this inside. The rain is getting heavy." Her voice leveled out from a whisper to a low tone. "Grab your things."

Noreen's discomfort at betraying her sister's trust didn't last long. The second their mother left the car she took the handles of the pastry bags in one hand and unbuckled. "Too bad. I know you were probably hoping for a lot of attention and sympathy at school. Stop being so dramatic and self centered, for all our sakes. It's getting old. And lame."

"You suck," Hannah said with tears brimming in her eyes, cheeks blotchy with rage. "Thanks for nothing, drama queen," She muttered under her breath before the sniffles kicked in. The rain completely shielded the view from the windows at this point. There were no clouds to offer a distraction and even the lull she always felt at the beauty of wet earth and wind was shaken.

"Takes one to know one," Noreen retorted snidely.

.
.
.

2

Dahlia felt her heart splinter into a dozen pieces after hearing what Hannah had let some kids believe. She knew her daughters were having difficulty with their father's absence. She reminded herself that letting people assume he was dead was not the same as wishing he were dead.

Right?

She was in her bedroom, shucking off her raincoat and changing into sweats. The master suite was tucked into its own corner of their spacious two-story home. Outside her bedroom window was a small balcony overlooking their yard. A vintage vanity and chair stood in the opposite corner, close to the armoire gifted to her by her mom almost 20 years ago. The rain continued to pour down - the sky was weeping the tears she couldn't let fall. She would let them fall eventually, in prayer, relinquishing all her frustrations, fears, and despair to God. She removed her jewelry, watch, and headscarf. She loosened her hair and combed her fingers through the tightly wound strands. She sat down on the vanity chair, leaning her head into her hands. She swallowed her anxiety and sighed.

Dead, she thought. Gone and never to return to this life again. Her face lifted and looked into the mirror. A solitary lamp was on a few feet away on top of an end table. The afternoon was gloomy and her gaze shifted from the shadowed carpet to the window. She had remembered to close it just before leaving. Her gaze fell again. Her brilliant blue eyes felt heavy. Dahlia had realized weeks ago that the one thing she and her girls required was some serious dialogue that was continuous and binding. She knew there was a chance she could suffocate them with so much conversation, but as long as they were talking, connecting, she felt better.

Her fingers massaged the back of her head and the light brown waves eased down her shoulders. Her wedding ring caught a few strands and she hastened to pull them out. She focused on the ring.

It was a simple emerald cut diamond on a rose gold band. Her initial ring had belonged to her mother-in-law, customarily given to the oldest son. Her husband asked if she wouldn't mind keeping that on for a few months. She hadn't. The newness of their relationship and the excitement that built as the wedding approached caused her to leave a lot of her reservations behind. Her husband's family ring nestled a large ruby. It was too big on her long and dainty fingers, but the delicate Indian design didn't welcome any resizing.

She had worn the ruby ring around her neck for several years after her husband gifted her the ring of their own choosing on their first Valentine's Day as a married couple. Over the past few months, however, she had slowly gotten rid of anything that felt weighty - spiritually and physically – and she had removed the heirloom necklace she wore daily and put it into a velvet lined case in her dresser drawer. She would take it out when her in-laws came.

Dahlia's hand moved to pick up her hairbrush. A framed family photo stood next to it. Taken just five years earlier, their wide smiles doubled the aches in her heart.

Adam was five years older than Dahlia. When they married, she was in her second year of college, and he had already been accepted into medical school in Arizona, a few hours from home. Their families had grown up together, and she had been sweet on him for some time. He had the funniest jokes, the most dazzling smile, and a heart made of gold. They met often at community events and would attend the same weekend schools and summer programs. Needless to say, their paths crossed often. Their parents weren't close family friends, but they knew each other well enough to feel comfortable that both she and Adam had their heads on straight enough to marry fairly young. His mother had had reservations, worried about his career and the financial strain, but he calmed her with the same charm he used on his classmates who had voted him class president during high school.

After brushing her hair, Dahlia took a few moments to reflect on the picture of her precious family. Hannah was snuggled into her dad's side and next to her Noreen grinned. These days, Noreen was more polished in her behavior so she didn't get to see many unabashed grins. The girls in the picture were wearing the same dresses, something they would balk at doing now.

Sometimes they even balked at wearing the same *color*, Dahlia noted. As if anyone was going to see them at two different school campuses and realize it.

One of the nurses at her clinic had warned her that this phase would come. The almost inevitable next stage in their relationship: *frienemies*.

Shaking her head, she mused at how things had changed in just a few years. Eventually, she left her bedroom and went downstairs.

The staircase wound into a semi-circle and she entered the den, looking towards their breakfast nook.

Hannah was sitting on a breakfast stool with a notebook and pen. She had loved to draw from an early age and resorted to it whenever her emotions became too intense to control. Teenagers, Dahlia recalled from her own phases of growing up, were all about intense emotions. She knew that the same unrest that plagued her each day was probably magnified in the girls. Had she neglected them? No, she answered herself. She knew she had exhausted every single effort imaginable, making sure she and the girls didn't fall apart as their father was hospitalized.

Hannah was especially close to him. She was born in their fifth year of marriage, when schedules were tight and hours were grueling with work and study. She bubbled with instantaneous laughter anytime he approached. When he'd be half asleep, she would lay curled around his head like a cat. If he started snoring, she'd chortle with delight and he'd come out of his sleep with a smile on his face.

Noreen had taken over setting the table for their prearranged chocolate session. Under the circumstances these days, Dahlia really appreciated Noreen's composure and ability to function in helping out. Dahlia mused that she often appeared stronger than she was herelf.

Under their kitchen island were a few straw picnic baskets. As the girls were growing up, she and Adam had found some time to make picnics in the park or pick up the girls from school for surprise trips on otherwise ordinary days. Noreen peeked into two of the baskets and found tools for knitting in one and some coupons in the other, along with some packets of hot chocolate. So much for her mom's fancy new recipe. Hannah had ruined that.

She ripped open the small squares and dumped the soft brown powder into a saucepan. She added milk and a sprinkling of cinnamon. As it heated, she stirred it absentmindedly. Hannah observed her from beneath her lashes, still annoyed that her trust had been betrayed.

Dahlia watched them quietly for a few moments. She could see what Hannah was doodling. She was sketching clouds again. Clouds above mountains. The tips merged into the sky and the wisps of differently shaped ellipses circling in the horizon. The ones at the bottom of her sketch were smaller and closer together, carrying each other's weight, merging together. As the width and sturdiness expanded, Hannah sketched those higher on her page. The ones that seemed closer in proximity were more solid.

As simple as it was, Dahlia was grateful Hannah had an outlet to express things she was obviously not discussing with anyone.

Noreen was more assertive when it came to difficult situations. She was always finding ways to overcome obstacles and find solutions to the problems at hand. Whether that be organizing tutoring groups for an especially difficult math class at school or being the one to make sure the trash got taken out every Thursday in Adam's absence.

Ever since Noreen had started high school, Dahlia had begun shifting domestic responsibilities onto her shoulders. She was trying to get her accustomed to being able to live independently. Her own mother never allowed anyone in the kitchen, so at first Dahlia had depended heavily on Adam's quick work in the culinary department to keep from starving. Eggs were his favorite, and generously buttered toast. Once the girls came into their lives, she became more accustomed to putting together an adequate meal and could now safely say she was a pretty decent chef.

"Girls," Dahlia spoke, angling their attention towards her. She gestured for her daughters to join her at the table. Noreen poured three mugs of hot chocolate and brought them over on a tray.

Noreen had chosen their array of mugs carefully. Again, Dahlia found herself comforted by her daughter's thoughtful addition of small comforts to the stressful atmosphere.

One was a hot pink mug with roses, obviously for herself. Another one for Hannah, something Adam had bought her when she'd first started track, with a handle in the shape of a running shoe. Dahlia's mug was one with best mom scribbles all around it, from the girls' grade school years.

Hannah took the pastries out of the boxes and arranged them at the table, then she sat down and hunched over her mug. Silence reigned for a few minutes as the women stared into the somber brown of their warm drinks. What seemed like a comforting treat had turned into an unappetizing but-much needed distraction from looking at one another.

"Hannah," Dahlia said. She reached her hand over so that it covered her daughter's. "I know that it wasn't your intention to let people think your father is dead. What makes me uncomfortable is that you're giving up appearances that he even exists. Which he does. Very well and alive. I see him every single day and each day I'm there, I let him know that you girls are giving him your love, support, and prayers."

A wave of guilt and regret pulsed through Dahlia's veins. The decision for Adam to volunteer with Doctors Without Borders in Syria had been made together, and no one could have foreseen the shocking eruption of the violence, but wasn't there somewhere else he could have gone instead? Was there ever really a right time to take a risk and venture into unknown regions of the world? Should she have pushed harder for a delay in his trip, maybe a few more years when they could both have gone together after the girls left for college?

The girls understood their father had been hurt in an armed conflict at the clinic where he was stationed with two other doctors. The organization helicoptered him out to Europe and he eventually made it back home, still needing hospitalization and treatment for his injuries.

Hannah interrupted her mother, emotions unraveling. "I'm sorry. It was wrong of me. I'm going to start making an effort again." She nodded for emphasis.

"Hannah," Dahlia sighed. "This isn't about me making you feel forced into something you don't want to do." *Though that would be nice*, Dahlia thought to herself. "The past few weeks have been turbulent. Your father came back with very serious injuries and that took a toll on his body...and his mind," she added quietly.

"I know," Hannah replied, bleakly. "I'm not being forced into it."

Noreen scoffed into her drink and Hannah gave her a quick glare.

"It's a situation none of us were ready for, but that's what life does, sometimes. And everyone copes in different ways and at a different pace " She hoped Noreen would let that last tidbit sink in and ease up on Hannah.

Hannah took a slow sip of her hot chocolate. The mug, with its running shoe handle, was vibrantly colored in bright blues and yellow. Adam had a knack for getting the girls adorable gifts and they were obviously cherished.

Dahlia looked between Hannah and Noreen. Hannah was tall, awkward sometimes, but always had a dreamy look in her eyes. Her head was in the clouds, and it showed. It probably wasn't easy to accept that their vibrant, loving father had returned a broken man with blank stares and minimal words. She herself had been floored by the changes, but after the initial breakdown, she braved forward, hoping that somehow with the right treatment, things would be fine again. Her medical brain was riddled with research and statistics about post-traumatic stress disorder, therapy, risk of infections, the length of time wounds took to heal, and almost everything under the sun that was relevant to her husband getting better. She couldn't sit on the sidelines, but since there wasn't much tangible benefit she could offer, she would try to prepare as best as possible.

Hannah's eyes welled with tears. "It's so hard," she choked out. "I miss him and I want him to be fine again. I just want him to be fine again. This isn't fair." At the last word, her tears fell with force.

Dahlia rose from her seat and pulled Hannah into a hug, holding her tightly.

"Fair or not, it's happening." Noreen quietly inserted her two cents as Hannah cried.

"Yes, Noreen, it's happening," Dahlia agreed, making her tone slightly firmer. She hadn't grown up with sisters, but everyone said this sparring came with the territory during their teenage years. Maybe they would calm down when they hit their thirties.

That's something else one of the nurses at her clinic said.

She continued without commenting further on Noreen's interjection. "We have to slow down and think about how at least we have him back. He's alive, Hannah." She spoke intensely, lifting Hannah's chin in her hand. "*Alive.*"

Hannah nodded, holding her gaze for a few moments. She broke the eye contact and looked down, continuing to sniffle.

"A lot of people there weren't so lucky."

Dahlia thought of the team of nurses and doctors that had gone to that part of the world. The three month trip was supposed to fulfill their dream as doctors, helping those who otherwise couldn't get medical aid. The civil war that broke out, the anarchy, everything crumbled around them so quickly.

Hannah wiped her face with the sleeve of her sweatshirt. She sniffed and deliberately didn't look at Noreen. Noreen was private about her tears and always scoffed at Hannah's melodramatic meltdowns, as she called them. She saw that her mother's eyes were warm and shining with unshed tears. The rock at the bottom of her gut lightened just the tiniest.

Dahlia kissed Hannah on her head and sat back down between the two girls.

Noreen was silent. The air was thick with unspoken fears and silent prayers.

"It's getting dark," Dahlia noticed. "We should pray and heat this hot chocolate up again. I wanted to share this with you guys later when I had a definite date, but the doctors said by as early next week, they're hoping Dad'll be ready to come home." She gave a tight but encouraging smile to the girls. "At least that's one step more than where we started today."

Thunder rumbled further away. The storm had moved past them without anyone noticing.

.
.
.

3

Noreen fumbled with the combination on her locker. She was in a hurry to make it to her first yearbook committee meeting. Noreen had started an international book club at the beginning of the year, but that didn't generate any interest aside from herself and a couple of classmates from World Literature class. She decided to forgo that and put her efforts into something that was already running and hoped that being on the yearbook committee would add to her growing list of activities to put on college applications. Athletics didn't catch her interest and theater seemed to just waste time. Band was full of kids who were rumored to just be hooking up with each other before or after practice, and Noreen didn't want to go near that. The yearbook committee was inviting and invigorating. At least all the emails she received from its coordinator were enthusiastic. She could learn new skills by dabbling in graphic design, and the tech stuff looked like it would be fun to figure out.

Her phone buzzed. She had set her alarm to alert her two minutes before meeting time. Her locker finally rattled open and she exchanged textbooks for a few notebooks. With expert swiftness, she switched her phone camera to selfie mode and made sure there was nothing in her teeth from her quinoa and organic mango smoothie lunch.

Noreen couldn't stand the smell of the cafeteria, so she sat outside near the library where the school set up benches and small tables for upperclassmen to study or have lunch. There weren't too many tables and oftentimes it was too sticky and humid under the Texas sun to enjoy it, but Noreen tried as much as possible to catch some fresh air in the middle of the day.

Plus, vitamin D was so crucial to protecting against random diseases and conditions, Noreen would remind herself when the sun became a bit too bright. There was always a mini bottle of sunscreen in her messenger bag to avoid burns. When she went through her avoiding natural sunlight phase in fear of putting herself at a high risk of skin cancer or something else that would sound as dastardly to deal with, she noticed that lack of vitamin D was making her tired and lethargic.

Granted, she noticed because her mom wouldn't stop nagging at her for lounging around so much more than she regularly did.

Still, it was good to be informed.

Approving her appearance, she turned her phone off and slammed the locker shut, dashing along the hallway. Students crowded the maze of corridors, anxious to catch buses home, run to a practice, or linger by their lockers with friends.

Suddenly, she slammed right into a body. A much larger one that grunted.

"Hey," the larger body exclaimed, shoved an inch by her slight frame.

Taken aback and slightly embarrassed, she mumbled, "Oh, sorry."

A spark of recognition flooded into her mind and she continued to explain, "I obviously need to look where I'm going. Are you okay? Keith, right?"

"Uh, yeah," he responded. "It's cool."

Keith Richmond. He was a football player and was in a couple of her extracurricular classes. He was taller than her, of course, with wide shoulders. After his initial surprise, he smiled.

"Where are you off to in such a hurry," he asked with a teasing light in his eyes.

"Oh," Noreen said again. She was becoming a little flustered because the seconds kept ticking away. Her one minute alert for yearbook committee was probably going to go off in less than thirty seconds.

"Sorry," she said, shaking her head. "I have to run. There's a yearbook committee meeting I need to be at right now."

"Like right now, right now, right?" he asked, still smiling. "I actually signed up for that, too. The athletics department wants us football players to be well-rounded instead of just meat heads running around on a field. Can you believe it?" he asked. "Expecting athletes to do more than just toss a ball around and knock each other over?"

Noreen's brows furrowed at his self-deprecating comments and she murmured an unintelligible response.

Keith laughed and elaborated. "I'm just joking. Not about being in the committee, but the other part. I can be a team player on and off the field," he joked. "Can I tag along with you?"

"Sure," she replied hastily. "We should hurry though. First impressions and all that. The last thing you want is to chalk up as a slacker and be volunteered for boring assignments, right?"

"Totally," he agreed. They moved along the hall amiably. "Their email did make the yearbook stuff sound cool. Probably cooler than it really is."

Noreen remembered the email from the yearbook committee a few weeks ago. "It was really flashy," she admitted, dropping her phone in her messenger bag and adjusting it over her hip after the one minute alert went off on her phone. "Still, it beats other things going on here, and you want to rack up as many club involvements while you have the chance."

"I haven't ventured into much outside of football. There's that foreign language and auto clinic stuff that's basically required which was kind of a drag. I remember seeing you there."

"Yeah," she acknowledged, recalling his face from the masses in the classrooms she had been in over the years. "The auto clinic wasn't so bad. At least I can change a flat tire now. Maybe." Pursing her lips and angling around more people, she mulled. "As long as there's someone around who weighs like 50 pounds more than me to get the jack thing to move."

Keith laughed. "You looked like you were levitating on it."

"I might as well have been," Noreen responded, laughing too. She was taking two steps to each one of his.

"You seem pretty brainy," he continued to tease. "I don't think you'll get any easy and boring assignments for this yearbook gig. I remember pre-calculus over the summer. Crosby with the nose gave all that extra credit for re-teaching a lesson to the class. No one did it but you. You seem pretty outgoing and involved for openly being so...different." He gestured towards the scarf on her head. "Is that something...," he paused to find the right word.

"Religious," she finished up with some clarity. Slightly turned off now since he attributed her scarf to something that would make her seem different, she responded in her usual way. He probably would have said the word *weird* had he not paused and corralled his brain cells together.

"Yup, she explained extra casually. "It's a religious thing for me, to wear a scarf on my head. So, I'm Muslim. Abrahamic religion. Islam. The usual keywords on Google search engines."

Keith laughed. "Well," he responded, "I figured it was something religious. Either that or you lost your hair to cancer like my aunt. She wore scarves for awhile too, but hers weren't as cool as yours."

Noreen was flattered and slightly ashamed for thinking he was dumb for a few seconds. She took pains to look unique and fashionable, making sure her hair was covered with bright scarves that coordinated with her outfits and accessories. Just because the impression people had of Muslim women was of stifled, darkly-clothed clones didn't mean she had to fit that stereotype. Instead, she embraced her individuality in observing her hijab.

She remembered getting called a lot more names than *different* some time ago, and reminded herself to stop being so annoyed at people trying to ask questions nicely.

"Hey, Noreen," called out a familiar voice. Noreen turned around and saw Leslie, a girl from her science lab, a few feet behind her and Keith. "Can you send me your notes from last Friday?"

"Sure," Noreen said, taking out her phone and inserting a reminder with one hand for this evening to email notes over to her.

"How were your appointments?" Noreen inquired to her rotating lab partner. The fact that you didn't get stuck with the same person all semester was such a relief. "You didn't miss much. The frog eggs will come later."

Leslie grinned, her teeth shiny and straight under a nose scattered with freckles. "Except that my mouth feels slimy, great. Can't wait to enjoy life without the wires."

Noreen laughed, tucking her phone away again. "I can't imagine."

"Thanks, Noreen," Leslie passed her and Keith, still smiling with her newfound dental freedom. "See you with the eggs later."

Keith continued to walk next to Noreen, hands in his pockets, nodding to a few of his own friends as they made their way around the building.

Not talking much now, they reached the room together. People were still filtering in and out. Noreen was habitually punctual, but even she had to concede from time to time that not many people took promptness as seriously as she did, so she tried not to be as aggravated when she wound up on time somewhere but by herself. Students loitered around the desks and Noreen took a seat a couple of rows behind the first. She was eager, but not nerdy eager enough to sit in the front row.

Noreen made it a habit to be friendly and outgoing. She loved working in groups and meeting new people, and had a great time having her hand in different projects. She thrived on social activity and academic pressure. The yearbook committee would be awesome too, she thought to herself. Seeing that the meeting wasn't going to begin exactly on time, Noreen arranged her notebooks and pen on the desk. Her phone was dressed in a bright yellow cover and she used the selfie mode camera feature again to discreetly check on her *hijab*.

No wrinkles or loose ends, she observed, except the ones that were positioned there for a wavy effect. Noreen was pleased with herself.

Veronica Louis was the committee president and she gave a quick welcome. "Okay guys," she announced. "We have a few new team members this quarter. Welcome Keith, Felicia, and Noreen." She pointed out the trio to the seasoned members and continued. "Since we're well into the school year, we're really excited that ya'll took some time out of your already busy schedules to respond to our call for more helping hands. Let's just jump right into what we've got going on after quick introductions."

As Veronica spoke, Noreen couldn't help but take a few more peeks at the other new girl on the yearbook committee.

Felicia looked familiar. Like, really familiar. Noreen stared at her for a few awkward moments where she was seated diagonally from her before realizing why her brain had made the connection. She remembered that she had seen Felicia at Winthrop Medical Center. Sometimes they would walk into the psych ward as Noreen and her mom were leaving. Saturdays were family-filled days. Once or twice they'd exchanged nods of acknowledgement.

There were five other people on the team that gave brief statements about themselves, obviously bored and uninterested in making introductions again. Each had an established rapport with the rest and they ignored Felicia and Noreen, establishing a silent social hierarchy.

Veronica handed out some assignments and then asked the committee members to work individually or help out with an ongoing project. The budget and graphics were already handled. Only the mundane tasks of editing and getting quotes from students and faculty were up for grabs. Felicia signed up for editing and Noreen paused. She thought editing would be pretty boring.

Quotes it would be, she surmised, and jotted her name down on the task sheet.

Keith put his name down for student and faculty quotes right after she did. He smiled again and asked, "Is it okay if we tag team on this? Two heads are better than one."

"Sure," murmured Noreen. In the back of her mind she was glad to have someone to get the athletics department quotes. "You can do all the jock stuff."

"Yeah, for sure," he agreed. "I don't think I made a lasting impression on any faculty unless they were begging me not to fail, but I got the sports people down."

"That'll be awesome," Noreen said. While they were both sitting down, she was able to almost angle her gaze at eye level with his. "Divide and conquer."

"Divide and conquer," he agreed.

Well, that'll be a relief, she thought to herself. She barely knew which way the gym was, much less anything about the teams, players, and coaches.

Quickly, she searched on her phone for the directory of faculty and department heads. By the time she had taken some screen shots, the meeting was closing up.

Veronica gave a few more instructions about keeping in touch through emails and their committee group on the school Blackboard program. The old members ignored Felicia and Noreen as they filed out as a group, but Keith got roped into their midst.

The two girls looked at each other and shrugged. Neither acknowledged being snubbed. Noreen smiled at Felicia, hoping to make up for the awkward stare at the beginning of the meeting.

Her phone buzzed with a message alert just then, so she grabbed it.

"Hey," Felicia started to speak, hesitantly. "Do you, like, volunteer at the hospital or something?"

Noreen started to reply, now fiddling with her phone and skimming text messages. "I don't really volunteer there." One text was just from her mom checking in. She looked up again, answering, "Not officially volunteer. Sometimes the nurses will ask me to do stuff because my mom deliveries babies there, and then I'm stuck carting around kids' books to the little library or taking cookies to new moms. Sometimes there's like a never-ending stream of babies," she added, rolling her eyes.

The girls grimaced at each other at the thought of childbirth.

"I go there with my mom and sister on the weekends, too," Noreen continued. The two were alone in the room now. "I thought you looked familiar. We've probably run into each other." She took a deep breath, rushing to finish. "My dad came back from working with a medical team in Syria a couple of months ago and had a lot of injuries because his clinic was attacked. So we're like always there visiting him." She hastily added, "Until he gets home. Hopefully soon."

Felicia seemed relieved and excited. Her nose was freckled, just like Leslie's, and she pushed a few strands of dyed red hair behind her ear to reveal an entire lobe full of piercings. Her words bubbled on top of each other. "My brother had a nervous breakdown or something and he's been there full time for about a week. They're putting him on meds to calm him down. Is your dad on medication, too? Those are some intense drugs, right?"

Noreen nodded. "Yeah," she murmured. "It can get pretty crazy." She looked down at her phone again blindly, not really wanting to continue the conversation, but feeling bad for Felicia.

Come to think of it, she felt bad for herself, too.

"My mom's really into those group therapy sessions. I'm not sure if you guys have gone yet."

Felicia frowned. "Uh, yeah, no. Those are so boring."

Noreen understood. "The Kool-Aid stuff they have there doesn't help either."

"Very vomitrocious."

The girls fell silent again. Noreen thought about her dad and hoped that when he was home, things could go back to the way they were. Nausea rolled its threatening head whenever she thought back to the first few days at the hospital.

The frightening reality of what could have happened to him and the unpromising changes in his condition were tough to swallow. But, as she had said to Hannah during one of her many meltdowns, feelings don't change reality.

The hallway clamor had calmed down, and a faint sound of wheels reached the room. Probably the cleaning crews, Noreen surmised.

There was always a fresh smell of cleaning detergent to walk into on school mornings. Noreen didn't divulge that she enjoyed the lemony fresh scent of detergent to anyone, though. She knew that would be a bit much.

Felicia stood up and grabbed her backpack, which had a popular crown and "Keep Calm" slogan printed on it. Her sleeves were fashionably frayed.

"If you need help editing, let me know," Noreen told her, also getting up. "Sometimes I'm up late doing random stuff and I don't mind helping. Shoot me a text."

"Yeah, I will. We could even work on some stuff if we're at the hospital at the same time. We all go once a day, taking turns, and then go together on weekends." Felicia's voice was slightly forced and Noreen couldn't tell if she needed the distraction at the hospital or was just being overly nice.

They exchanged numbers and headed out of the classroom. Felicia, along with the half dozen piercings along her earlobe, wore several rings. One featured a miniature cross design and another was a rose. Jewelry could tell you a lot about a person. Noreen loved to accessorize, and since her mom had been on a minimalist kick for some years now, she got to utilize the classier pieces of her collection. Felicia's rings reminded her that she hadn't borrowed any rings in ages. Maybe she'd browse through her mom's armoire tonight.

"He's my twin brother," Felicia remarked, a little abruptly.

Noreen stayed quiet, shifting out of her own thoughts, and waited for her to elaborate.

Felicia fell silent again and continued walking to the double doors leading outside at the end of the corridor.

Once out of the building, Noreen squinted at the bright Texas sun and walked to her car in the vast student parking lot. Felicia loped around in the other direction. Most of the students had emptied out but several dozen cars remained, belonging to those who had after school activities or tutoring. Not much socializing happened off school hours unless there was a big event like a dance or a game. Then it seemed like the entire school turned up - and then some.

Noreen unlocked her car absentmindedly and gazed around. A hint of a breeze played with the tail ends of her scarf and cooled the back of her neck. She was already getting sweaty and hadn't been out for more than a minute.

Texas sunshine, she thought, shaking her head. Love it or hate it, it will be what it is. Unapologetically blazing and blinding. The rays were sharp and obtrusive, almost violent in their energy.

Strangely, she felt strengthened and empowered by soaking up its rays. It may be the same sun that lit up the entire world, but there was something magnificent in the powerful way it scorched things at this tip of the country.

Hannah was definitely the type to busy herself by doodling about clouds that would hide the sizzling beams of light. There were others, Noreen knew as she breathed in deeply, that could absorb the radiance of the sun and embrace it completely. She would fight off the clouds with all her might.

A blond head caught the edge of her view several yards away once she maneuvered her bag off her body and tossed it into the passenger seat.

Keith, she realized, was parked a few rows behind her and she noticed his football team jacket again. She loved the sun but she wasn't ridiculous enough to wear a heavy jacket during peak heat hours. He was about to get into his car when he looked up and their eyes locked. She reminded herself to switch the disdain and judgement off.

He waved and she acknowledged him, keeping it casual by just lifting her arm instead of waving back. He then shouted over the scattered cars, "Blue is my favorite color," pointing to his head, referring to her scarf.

Noreen responded with an exaggerated thumbs up. She made a mental note to think about wearing blue at the next meeting. Not because of what he said, she affirmed to herself, but because blue was actually *her* favorite color.

⋮

4

The nurse stepped away from Adam as she checked the thermometer for his temperature. "Dr. Jamal," she announced to him as he lay in bed. "You are doing just fine and dandy today! I'm sure you're excited to be getting on home to your beautiful girls after so much time in the hospital. Bless your soul."

His soul, he thought.

Lifeless. Pointless. Aimless.

Blessed.

Is that what she said?

Didn't she know blessings were something he couldn't have.

Shouldn't have.

A defeated soul.

His defeat.

Her aging hands quickly wrapped up the equipment reading his vital signs and wheeled around to leave the room. Her hair curled around her ears and her heart-shaped earrings sparkled a bright, cheerful red. They matched her sparkling red nails.

Adam didn't do anything to confirm what she'd said.

He stared at the wall.

Her bright earrings bled into his vision.

They bled into the wall behind her.

The wall in front of him.

Mostly, he stared at the ceiling.

But his upper body was elevated.

Aching despite the medication.

Miserably.

Angrily.

His eye twitched.

Teeth gritted.

The arch of his feet cramped.

Sometimes, the nurses came and spoke in jolly voices. Instead of sounding warm and comforting, their chipper voices buzzed in his ears.

The buzzing would wane.

High and low.

Deep and intense, pounding inside his head.

Sometimes. They would itch. The voices.

In his mind.

He wished they'd stop calling him Dr. Jamal.

The doctor he had been was left somewhere else, in another part of the world.

The hands he saw now held no healing.

Held no help.

Held nothing but defeat.

Adam was angry at that person.

Dr. Jamal.

He let an entire team of doctors down.

Brilliant men. Brilliant women.

Bright eyed. Dedicated. Optimistic.

He let innocent people down.

Small ones. Old ones.

Bodies. Everywhere.

No medical degree to wield in defense.

Everything that he was made up of as a person had failed those in need.

As a doctor, had failed those in need.

As a person, had failed those in need.

A million and one cotton balls swirled inside his head.

He was still slow to process things. Quick to feel irritation.

It was easier not to respond.

Silence drove people away from him faster.

The people made him angry, when he was lucid enough to acknowledge his emotions. The medications and their side effects made him angry.

God made him angry.

Adam made himself angry.

He tried to take a deep breath and felt twinges against his sides.

Those were infuriating.

Feeling pain. When so many felt nothing at all now.

He heard the doctors.

His recovery from broken ribs was slow.

But healing.

His ankle was almost fine again.

A limp. He managed it irritably.

There were some scars behind his legs and on the back of his shoulders from debris that exploded every which way.

Bullets.

Explosions.

Madness. Panic.

Bleeding into the wall.

In front of him.

Behind him.

The whole world was flying in chaos, then. Adam didn't understand the injuries until much later. By then, his heart had screamed and wailed in his chest.

Beating its bloody pumping fists against the broken ribs.

Agonized. Haunted and enraged.

Angry. Frightened.

Angry.

The wheels carrying the nurse's portable blood pressure machine clashed suddenly against the door with a loud clanking sound.

It echoed. Loudly. He could almost swear. Almost.

He could almost swear he felt his brain tremble.

Shaking forcefully.

Close to shattering.

The panic. Startling and skipping into his heart.

Losing rhythmic beat. Inhale. Exhale.

Can't. Fully. Be calm.

The nurse finally exited the room. With her red earrings.

Blood red.

In the wall in front of him.

Behind him.

The ceiling. They all mocked and reminded him.

Failure. Whispers of clanking prattled around in his ears.

Between his forehead and his eyes.

Rattling. Slowly. Itching to consume him.

Instead of calming down, his heart beat faster and felt like it was going to jump out of his chest.

There was a storm a few weeks ago. It rattled and roared. It had only lasted a short time, but each second was an agonizing battle. It began with lightning and rolling thunder in the distance. Explosions he knew were headed his way.

The rain started soon after.

Started and roared into a fury, mimicking bullets against the window pane.

Pelting threateningly.

Reminding him.

The thunder was explosive.

His eyes were wide against his stark white face. He lay in his darkened hospital room, focused on one ceiling tile.

Frozen then.

Frozen now.

"Adam, you have a classic case of post-traumatic stress disorder," Dr. Finland explained two months ago. He had started off referring to him as Dr. Jamal like the rest of the hospital staff but quickly switched to Adam. "Your nightmares, the inability to sleep, even your self-blame. You know this. You're a physician yourself. Let's work on methods of exposure therapy to limit falling into the emotional traps of your symptoms and get a handle on the situation."

Exposure therapy, Adam recalled during the storm. He stared at one ceiling tile, focusing and practicing a way to keep his mind from slipping through.

Concentrating.

By the time the thunder passed, his body was jittering uncontrollably, layered in a sheen of sweat. Jaw clenched, he breathed heavily through his nose and stifled moans of agony, recalling the scenes in Syria. He was helpless then, and he was even more helpless now.

He had failed everyone.

A sharp, quick shot blasted into the room.

The door.

Adam stifled a shout.

The door. He focused.

It was still intact.

He wasn't at the clinic.

Dr. Finland poked his head into the room. Adam was already gripping the side bar, stressed from the nurse's departure. His grip tightened after the knock, going unnoticed by the doctor.

"Well I can safely give you the green light to go home, my friend. There are a lot of prescriptions that are probably safer to take than avoid for the time being. You responded well to Prazosin, mainly because it put you to sleep and calmed the adrenaline down during your anxiety and flashbacks."

He stood at the foot of the bed and flipped through a couple of sheets on a clipboard. "Sleep is very, very crucial on your road to recovery," he continued. "Your brain has to rest. The anti-depressants will get you geared up to concentrate and there are anti-anxiety medications that we might put you on depending on how well you do at home."

After mentioning home, he looked up at Adam, who stared back stoically and smiled. "Don't look so glum. Those shouldn't be for long term, and to be frank, Adam, it's a tricky process of finding the right cocktail of medication and dosage to get you back on your feet like you were before all this. We'll keep touching base depending on side effects and progress. You have medical leave, and I've discussed the details at length with your wife. I've gotten all the documents in order for you and ready for them to be dropped off at the administrative office on the sixth floor. Let them know if you have any questions. They send their best."

Adam nodded. His heart had leaped into his throat and clutched at his ability to voice a response. Deep breaths, he reminded himself.

Side effects.

Medicine.

Home.

He was going back home.

It was slowly sinking in.

The girls. His house. His wife.

Confined to another set of walls.

Walls that may reach out to him at night.

Smothering him.

Dr. Finland continued talking. He liked to provide abundant details for his patients so they felt like they were involved in the planning of their recovery. Whether or not they fully processed his information was another story.

Another knock at the door. Focusing on Dr. Finland rattling on with his details, Adam's panic had rolled away slowly. Now, his nerves became edgy and the sight of his beautiful, bright-eyed wife entering the room with a chipper *Salam* made him anxious. He felt trapped in the hospital room, panicked again at the thought of going home.

His daughters followed Dahlia inside the room and his worry deepened. He had hazy recollections of their time together just after he was flown back home. Knowing this deepened his concern about how he wouldn't be returning back to his family whole.

"Ready?" questioned Dahlia cheerfully. Her smile extended to her eyes as she looked at Adam. She turned to Dr. Finland and greeted him, too.

He could tell she was nervous. Even through the haze of medications and the agitation that swarmed in his mind, he felt her apprehensive gaze fixated at his face.

His face. Recalling the last time he'd looked in the mirror, he knew it was poofed up by drugs, but still gaunt.

Hannah and Noreen flanked their mother on either side and smiled at him.

"*As Salamu Alaikum*, Dad," they greeted in unison.

Adam couldn't continue to hold their gazes and looked down. He tried to respond in a normal tone. A spasmodic cough followed, his voice and throat both protesting at being urged into use.

"Let's go," he murmured, after the cough subsided.

"You're all set," Dr. Finland told Adam and his family. "Give me a call if you need anything."

"Thank you, Dr. Finland," Dahlia responded. Her plaid skirt was offset by a simple white cotton top. She looked unnatural to Adam. Wearing normal clothes in the hospital.

Dr. Finland finished up a few notations on his clipboard and rested a stack of papers at the foot of Adam's bed. "I'll let the nurse know you're ready."

Dahlia picked up the paperwork as she and the girls said goodbye.

Adam was quiet.

"Oh, look," Noreen said, trying to make light conversation. "You only have to wear a brace now, Dad. That shouldn't be so bad."

"You're right, Noreen." Dahlia. "You tripped over your new roller blades at the park and needed one, too, remember?"

"It was annoying not being able to walk around normally for a couple of weeks, but sitting on the sofa and watching TV helped," Noreen replied.

"We can stream some of dad's old favorites," Hannah plugged in.

"Absolutely," Dahlia agreed, excitedly.

"You could even slip in something you like, Mom," Noreen joked.

"Not *You've Got Mail*, please," Hannah said, pained.

"I don't know why you girls can't stand it. It's so cute. A guaranteed feel good."

"Um, sure Mom. If I needed a history lesson back to when computers were of the stone age."

"Noreen, not everything was at the tip of our fingers when Dad and I were growing up."

"Thank God for civilization, then."

"One day I'll school you on the dewy decimal system. Then you'll thank God."

"I'm okay, Mom. I'll take the Do-ey Google system and still thank God."

Hannah circled the conversation back to their dad. "Maybe we can pick up some dinner and make it a movie night tonight."

"Tonight may be too soon. Your dad seems tired."

All three women looked at Adam. He halfheartedly tried to smile, but it was more of a grimace.

"Yeah," Noreen agreed with their mom. "We can flip some coins about a movie marathon. Hannah will try to squeeze in *Lord of the Rings*. I can't stand it."

"You don't complain when Orlando Bloom is swinging from elephants," Hannah retorted.

"Okay, girls." Dahlia interrupted. "Let's get home and we can talk it over together with your dad. I'm sure he can't wait to be back!"

The last thing Adam wanted to do was sit at home and stare at running images on a screen. His favorites included movies like *The Godfather*. He knew he wouldn't be able to stomach that anymore.

After a few moments of no one saying anything, probably waiting for him to respond, he slowly eased his legs over one end of the hospital bed. He had worn comfortable pajama pants and a t-shirt for most of his stay at the hospital, but yesterday Dahlia had stopped off with some jeans and a polo.

His going home outfit she called it, teasing him.

At Dahlia's insistence, they all stepped in to help Adam stand.

"Stop," he said curtly, before Noreen and Hannah could grab an arm.

They retreated. Noreen put her hands behind her back and stood away, observing him with sympathetic eyes that Adam still couldn't look at for longer than a few seconds.

Hannah backed away until she hit the closed bathroom door and kept her gaze firmly on the ground.

Adam had a hard time looking her in the face at all.

Dahlia took over and reached in again, refusing to acknowledge his request.

"Honey, I'm going to grab your arm and put it around my shoulder, just to steady you," she dictated carefully to her husband.

"My ankle is fine. I can do it on my own," Adam said, his voice still raw and gruff. At least this time he didn't start coughing. He knew he'd caused both his daughters to retreat.

His heart pierced with pain.

Helplessness.

It was a different pain, just as intense.

He was failing again.

Losing.

Dread was inching into his mind about leaving the hospital.

There was no escaping it.

He leaned against his petite wife. She was stronger than she seemed, he knew.

"Hannah, hold the door open for when the nurse gets here," Dahlia requested firmly. Her left arm was locked around Adam's waist and the other secured his arm around her shoulders.

Noreen, closer to the door anyway, went ahead to open it and peer out for the discharge nurse.

Dahlia continued with her directions, giving orders to the hesitating members of her family. "Hannah, grab the duffel bag on the floor with your father's things and check the side table drawers in case anything needs to be packed up."

Her directions gave everyone purpose. Adam continued to lean on his wife, standing unsteadily. He would've collapsed on the floor if she hadn't shouldered his weight.

A different nurse came in, thanking Noreen for having the door open. "We're happy to see you go, Dr. Jamal," the nurse said with a kind, genuine smile. Her face was creased with laugh lines and her hair was rolled into a neat bun, with some frizzy hair escaping, sprinkled with gray, brown, and blonde strands.

She had worked extensively in the ER before switching to the psychiatric unit.

Adam remembered.

Shame prickled at the back of his neck.

It smirked at his memory.

Taunting.

Would she be smiling at you if she really knew.

So fond they are...all these people...of good ol' Dr. Jamal.

Worthless man.

    Worthless father.

        Worthless doctor.

Adam was too immersed in trying to hold up against the weight of his mind's whisperings to respond. He leaned off of his wife and, with the help of both her and the nurse, sat down.

The nurse began to wheel him into the hallway, chattering with Dahlia. The girls, upon Dahlia's instruction, gave the room another onceover and quickly followed the trio out.

He returned home.

⋮

Mom!" Noreen shrieked, aghast at the array of ready-to-use spice boxes lining the kitchen counter-top. "You're poisoning us! Look at the preservatives in here. I bet you can't even pronounce half of these words. Citric this, acid that. *Hydrolyzed SOY!*"

Her nostrils flared with agitation. "You can't even fathom the amount of cancerogenous molecules there are in there. You're a physician, for crying out loud!" Noreen's hands scraped the sides of her hair and she blew more frustrated breaths at the ceiling.

Dahlia was tuning her out and emptying another box of spices into a deep pot of steaming vegetables. "You're so right, sweetheart," she finally responded distractedly. Sometimes Noreen could turn into a little fire breathing dragon. Dahlia was used to her having tantrums over their food choices. Once or twice she even let Noreen get the groceries, but a $10 bag of organic pretzels on a weekly basis was not about to get her kids through college.

Dahlia's eyes narrowed over another bubbling curry. The colors swirled a bright orange with streaks of what might be chalked up as extra oil or another type of unknown seasoning that came inside the golden boxes she used as a lifeline for Indian recipes.

"Is something burning?" Hannah finally asked from her seat in the den, exaggeratedly sniffing the air.

Both Hannah and Noreen were in calf-length pajama bottoms and t-shirts. They'd nibbled on some fruit after waking up, but Dahlia had barricaded the kitchen and forbidden any other cooking or eating activity until her culinary operation was complete.

Dahlia was preparing a giant lunch for Adam's parents and family. After work yesterday, she'd stopped by the small Indian food market and loaded up on meat, vegetables, and spice boxes. The girls had attacked their list of chores last night as Dahlia dictated. Noreen only relented to her mother's task list with a plea of her own - not to be disturbed before noon.

"Nothing is burning yet," Noreen replied to Hannah. "Just a plot to poison her offspring." She vowed under her breath to avoid the chemicals in the lunch her mom was bent on feeding them.

Dahlia looked at the clock on top of the microwave. "Girls, please tidy up the kitchen and go upstairs to get into something appropriate." Her wrists flicked the stovetop burners off and covered the simmering pots with their lids. One of her fingers touched a burning rim. "Ouch!"

"Will we need the fire extinguisher this time, Mom?" Hannah teased. Dahlia knew the girls understood that cooking larger meals was a hassle for her. She tried to hide it as best she could, but there would always be a series of comments poking fun at her bumblings.

"Very funny, Hannah," Dahlia replied. *And wait until it's your own kitchen*, she smirked to herself. She tossed Noreen a roll of paper towels from a cabinet under the kitchen sink. "Please wipe down the countertops, Noori."

Noreen caught it with one arm and used the other hand to toss the empty spice boxes in the trash with complete disdain.

Dahlia's phone jingled a lively tune, signaling that there was an international call coming in. She wiped her grimy hands on her own pajama bottoms and answered happily.

"*Salam*, Mama!"

Dahlia's mother, Zyna, was too far away in Italy to come and see how Adam was doing. The concern in her mother's voice during each call the past few months prompted Dahlia to respond cheerfully and pleasantly, just as she had been doing with everyone who sympathized.

"Will Adam's family be staying with you for the entire weekend?" her mother asked after exchanging pleasantries. She began digging into the details of how Dahlia was getting ready for her in-laws visit. "I know they will be driving down in a series of cars like they usually do. His parents, siblings, their husbands and wives and children, too."

Indian families were generally big, and Adam's was no exception.

Dahlia responded "I didn't ask specifically." She gestured for Hannah to help her sister in the kitchen and threw a Noreen-approved microfiber cloth in her direction for good measure. As she walked through the den toward the staircase, she straightened out some trinkets on the bookshelf. "You know his mom becomes a little insulted if I ask about visit lengths. She wants to feel comfortable to come and go as she pleases, so I want to accommodate that. Especially because we argued over the phone about where he was going to stay after coming home. Since it's the whole brood that's going to come down though, I think they'll be at a hotel for the night. I've prepped the guest room on the main floor for his parents just in case they decide to stay longer."

"I know you've always been very nice to them," Zyna told her, referring to the relationship her daughter had with her husband's family. "And sometimes, it's hard to reach out and ask for help from people you're used to doing favors for, but maybe it won't be such a bad idea for Adam to stay with someone who can be with him around the clock."

There was a pregnant pause and Dahlia headed upstairs to argue with her mom without her daughters as audience.

"Mama," Dahlia gritted her teeth. "My husband is already back and staying in his own house with his wife and daughters. If he, for whatever reason, is possessed enough to want to stay at his parents' house and sleep in his old twin-sized bed in his tiny old bedroom as the chaos of all his brothers and sisters and nephews and nieces reigns around him, I'll consider it. In the meantime, we are going to take care of him right here."

"I doubt it's really his old twin-sized bed, Dahlia," her mother responded, amused.

"Mama," Dahlia argued. "I promise it is! You don't have to believe me, but if it ain't broken, they ain't replacing it - that's what Adam would say."

Her mother laughed on the other end. "Still, Dahlia. Think about it. Maybe a change of scenery and pace would jump start his incentive to get back to his routine."

Dahlia took a deep breath. She rubbed her temple with her free hand and opened the door to her bedroom with the other, phone snuggled between her ear and shoulder. "The girls are so excited he'll be home, Mama," she continued with deliberate patience. "It's been months! Months beyond the time we thought he would be away. I don't understand why people keep suggesting he be split apart from his family for more time."

Everything was beginning to seem as though it had stretched on for years and yet, at the same time, as if it was just yesterday that Adam left for Syria full of excitement and purpose. Not long ago when the girls were jovial and full of chatter and light all day long instead of being subdued and distracted. The thought made her shoulders droop as she cradled her cell phone in one hand, waiting for a response.

"Alright, sweetheart," Dahlia's mother eventually conceded. "I didn't mean to rile you up. Just keep an open mind in case Rehana brings it up again." Rehana, Adam's mother, was a very brusque woman who loved her children dearly and oftentimes showed her love through critical and grumbling comments.

"I'd love to see all of them, so send me a quick message on one of these messaging programs and I'll ask Maher to download Skype on our computer," she told Dahlia, referencing her second husband and trying to keep up-to-date with the new ways available to keep in touch. Overall, she thought she did a pretty decent job of regularly seeing her granddaughters and told Dahlia frequently what a blessing it was to have them at her fingertips.

"Sure, Mom," Dahlia smiled, looking forward to letting her mom "virtually" enjoy the chaos of Adam's big family. "They'll love it, too."

Dahlia knew the mannerisms were culturally different and, over time, had accepted the linguistic and habitual changes from her own upbringing. Her grandparents hailed from Spain, but her mother and aunts grew up in America and lived quiet and uncomplicated lives. Their family had shown resilience in maintaining their Islamic faith, the religion that had predominated in Spain centuries before. Somehow, generation after generation, their family held steadfast to their ideologies and practices despite political and social turmoil.

Zyna had been happily married until her husband passed away from a heart attack not long after Dahlia finished high school. It was after Zyna saw Dahlia settled with her own children that she opened her heart to remarrying and, ironically, wound up living in Europe.

Adam's parents had emigrated after they married and were prone to more traditional routines in which customs dictated plenty of festive occasions. Dahlia hadn't grown up with so many relatives or specific expectations, but tried to enjoy them. She took pains to make his family as comfortable as possible during their visits.

Customarily, Dahlia recognized, it wasn't rude of her to ask about the length of their visit, but because she and Adam's mother had stepped on each other's toes several times since his return from Syria, it was better to be safe than sorry. That afternoon's menu included lamb biryani, a few spicy curries, naan, and chai made with fresh mint leaves and cardamom pods. She also remembered to pick up her bakery order first thing after praying in the morning, quickly changing from her pajamas before leaving the house and slipping right back into them once she got home.

To Dahlia's credit, she was very resourceful in finding every shortcut possible, and all her gratitude went directly to the small rectangular boxes filled with assorted spices to add to meats and vegetables to create the perfect fusion of flavors for practically any Indian recipe. This always riled Noreen up, as she insisted they throw away boxed spices and only use organic and freshly ground ingredients.

Once Dahlia hung up the phone, she went back to the hallway and knocked on Adam's door. Hearing no response, she assumed he was sleeping and didn't enter.

Against Dahlia's better judgement, she had conceded to Adam sleeping in the guest room. Initially, he didn't say anything when she put his duffle bag in their bedroom at the foot of the bed the first night he came home. As dusk closed over them and the girls had retreated into their own rooms for the evening, though, Adam stood and said in a hoarse tone, "I can't be here, Dahlia."

At her protest, he continued haltingly. "I don't sleep well. I've gotten used to not having anyone around me. It would be easier for me to rest if I was in another room."

Dahlia pressed her lips together, swallowing hurt and anxiety remembering their conversation.

The girls came upstairs as she tucked away the painful memory. As usual, they were bickering.

"Go back and put the rag in the laundry room," ordered Noreen.

"You do it since you're so obsessed with where things belong," Hannah deflected the demand.

"Why would you just leave something on the kitchen table, knowing it'll become a cesspool of germs? You're disgusting."

"You're neurotic."

"Great comeback, genius. Move over," Noreen said, annoyance dripping from each word. "I'm showering first so you're nasty hair isn't all over the bathtub floor."

"You shed enough for both of us!"

Dahlia caught their attention by clearing her throat and put a finger against her lips to signal for quiet so their dad wouldn't be disturbed. Noreen immediately held up her hands in innocence and pointed at Hannah, mouthing that she had started it.

Hannah, fending off Noreen's blame by ignoring it, quickly darted into the bathroom and shut the door, leaving Noreen to further throw up her hands up in aggravation.

Dahlia sighed at their spat and retreated to her bedroom.

Shaking her head at Adam's silence and the girls' argument, she tossed her stained and smelly clothes into the hamper. It would take a lather, rinse, and a couple of repeats to wash away the fragrance of fried onions clinging to her hair.

An hour later, as she was setting the table, she heard Hannah race downstairs announcing that the relatives had arrived. Not a fan of dresses or skirts, Hannah wore palazzo pants as a way of dressing up, and a casual top gifted by one of her aunts on a family *Eid* holiday trip to the Grand Canyon.

She opened the front door and jetted out, the strings on her *hijab* gusting behind her. Generally, at home, none of the girls had to wear their scarves. Now with their extended family so vast and including relatives who weren't related by blood and cousins who were also becoming adults, it was religiously expected for them to cover. Not everyone chose to cover for extended male relatives, or cover at all for that matter, but Hannah and Noreen didn't have any qualms about it.

Dahlia felt like she got lucky with their compliant natures. She herself had found the act of covering an annoyance as a teenager. Most of her early education on the concept of *hijab* was that it was required out of modesty and other more patriarchal elements. As she got older, she realized it was to be recognized by those around her as a woman who believed in God. Despite her initial annoyance, she did enjoy distinguishing her choice of faith by appearance and felt more empowered. Her professionalism, mannerisms, and genuine character tied in with her religious garb and gave a refreshing perspective to those who weren't used to Muslims in their southern town.

Noreen followed Hannah out quickly and both girls shouted greetings to their grandparents, cousins, aunts, and uncles who piled out of their cars and minivans. Dahlia smoothed her skirt and adjusted her necklace from beneath her matching scarf before heading down herself. As she reached the door, she glanced behind her to an empty space. Usually, Adam was right there with them as they welcomed his family before they even entered the house. Her heart dropped a little more. She had secretly hoped that within a week he would be showing more signs of progress in reverting back to his jovial and social self. Instead, he had been reclusive and made almost no conversation unless prodded.

She put on a warm smile and stepped outside, extending her arms out in welcome as more arms wrapped around her in love, comfort, and relief that Adam's hospital stay was over. Dahlia reminded herself of that very fact as she cooed over new babies, exchanged greetings with more relatives, and felt her gaze warm over her giddy daughters delightfully exchanging jokes and teasing comments with their cousins.

After lunch was inhaled and the chai cooled in intricate teacups, Adam's mother lifted her hand to request silence. She and her husband's positions in their extended families were ones of high regard and deep respect. If anyone disagreed with what they had to say, they didn't make it obvious. Elderly relatives in Indian culture were deeply revered and honored. It was definitely different from Dahlia's upbringing, where she could still argue and joke around with her own older relatives, even partaking in heated discussions about politics.

The clamor and chatter of lunch quieted down. One of the babies chortled, amused at all the faces in the room and content with a belly full of rice and assorted snacks from everyone's plates.

Rehana addressed Dahlia directly. "Your father-in-law and I feel that Adam should come and stay with us for the next few weeks," she began. Her voice was firm.

Dahlia sighed internally, accepting her role of being the bad guy in this conversation. She was irked that this argument kept repeating since she had been on the phone with her mother-in-law just days ago. She tried to understand that Adam's parents were hurting on the inside, too. Seated a few feet from Rehana, Dahlia remained silent for the time being, resigned to hear her out. She felt Hannah's anxious stare against the side of her head and despite wanting to reassure her that no one was going to disrupt their family, she kept her eyes focused on Adam's mother.

Rehana continued, "We have several more people around in the family who could be with him constantly. You're at work for a good portion of the day and Adam is home alone. Given his condition, that's not ideal. There are medical facilities near us in Oklahoma City that he is familiar with, too. We're planning on driving back early tomorrow morning and would request that you pack some of his things."

The finalization of her statement was abrupt. Dahlia raised her eyebrows - the only hint of emotion she allowed herself to show. The request was merely a formality and Dahlia understood that Rehana expected her to comply, especially since she had given a timeline and made the delivery of her request in front of the entire family.

Noreen, Dahlia noticed from the corner of her eye, high-lighted by her neon green cardigan over a white maxi dress and white scarf, stood up. Her hands twisted and gripped each other in an effort to contain budding anxiety.

It wasn't often that her grandmother and mother were at odds. Almost never. This shift in their relationship's dynamic was awkward and discomfiting.

"No," Dahlia replied.

Silence was thick in the den. A number of Adam's siblings had settled on the well-cushioned sofas lining the wall across from their parents. Their kids were strewn across the room on chairs and on the floor, in various modes of pretending to ignore the adults emotional conversation, but listening intently for any hint of true drama.

Dahlia observed Hannah and Noreen looking nervously from their beloved grandparents to their mom. Each was in a different circle of cousins across the room, but their eyes found each other. Dahlia didn't smile at them, but she instinctively wanted to soothe their nervous trepidation.

Their cat Zuzu slipped between and around various chairs and leaped onto one of the bookshelves to a well-used napping spot between Adam's books about vintage cars and Dahlia's own collection of travel literature.

"If I need help, I will ask," Dahlia told her mother-in-law in a gentle tone. "You are more than welcome to stay and visit for as long as you'd like, but I'm not letting him go anywhere now that he's home."

Bilal, Adam's father, spoke sternly. "Dahlia, we almost lost our son in that crazy Doctors Without Borders stunt you two decided on, and we want him to return with us so that we may also care for him. It will be for the best if he comes with us!"

The finality of his statement was forced with heated emotion. He continued to speak, but Dahlia wasn't listening anymore.

Dahlia's ears muffled out the words and her temper kindled under the calm surface of her composed speech and posture.

"He already has his doctors here," she interrupted. Continuing, she added, "Also, my practice is being very flexible with our situation and I'm not gone for more than a few hours at a time. My on-call hours have been reduced as well."

"So if you have to deliver someone's baby in the middle of the night when Adam requires assistance, you'll have your young daughters manage," Bilal declared abruptly, disapproval lacing his tone.

One of Adam's brothers, Isaac, carefully interrupted.

"Maybe you should just ask Adam, Papa," he suggested kindly to his father. Rehana nodded, at least allowing her son consent about where he wanted to recuperate. Bilal shook his head, openly displeased at the ensuing tug of war.

They all looked at Adam. Dahlia felt protective over his condition and didn't want him pressured in any way. Adam had sat down on the lone recliner close to the bay windows in the den. The fatigue and wounds were obvious on his face and body. He was tired and dull-eyed. Lunch had been an excruciating ordeal, with lots of forced conversations, laced with the weight of his aging parents' concern.

"Adam," prompted his mother. "Sweetheart, wouldn't it be nice to stay with us for a few weeks as you recover? We've missed you terribly. The girls can visit on the weekends, and I'm sure there are some school holidays coming up."

The ridiculous suggestion of her daughters visiting Oklahoma City on weekends didn't escape Dahlia. She closed her eyes and sipped at her tea, praying for deliverance.

Adam blinked hazily. Rehana's heart was obviously aching for her son's distress. She had continued to smooth his hair throughout lunch and would whisper prayers under her breath and blow over him, practicing her own method of blessing his healing.

He spoke quietly, one shoulder rising and falling in a half-hearted shrug. "I'll stay here."

An uncomfortable silence reigned again. Rehana looked close to tears. Dahlia took this as a cue to carefully change the subject to upcoming holidays and different vacation spots they hadn't yet coordinated as a family.

"Let's aim to see each other again when Adam's ankle is fully recovered. Maybe a retreat with a cabin overlooking a lake?"

One of Adam's sisters-in-law agreed. "There are beautiful places in Wisconsin year round. I have some cousins near this place called Door County."

More joined in the conversation and Dahlia noticed Adam's parents look at each other, disappointed.

She hoped to provide something his parents could look forward to since they would leave here assuming they'd lost an argument. Adam's siblings gratefully continued her promoted discussion and the younger kids returned to their cell phones, chatter, and snacking on the remnants of lunch.

Dahlia spared Isaac a grateful glance and smiled at the girls, their relief palpable.

It occurred to her that before Adam's injuries, she would have done the same. Asked him his preference.

6

Track practice was set to begin in a few minutes. The girls were jogging out from locker rooms beyond the enclosed field. Hannah made it out early and was stretching. Her muscles were limber, used to the push and pull of drills. Her teammates were wearing cropped shorts she was in a full length tracksuit with a plain white scarf tucked into her track shirt. The coach had raised an eyebrow at first, but Hannah was obviously comfortable, so no issue was raised. Their coach was a middle-aged Asian woman who was still an avid marathon runner. She had been an assistant coach at the school and really took over the track team a couple of years ago. She had a passion for running that was almost blinding, but the girls enjoyed being motivated to run backed by her intense enthusiasm. Sometimes their team would practice before school started, which Hannah loved, but the majority complained made them feel gross the rest of the day.

The girls approached Hannah and settled down a little ways from her. It was nothing obvious, but the deliberate two feet of space was enough to mark the clique they had formed after the news of Hannah's father being alive was revealed. She went online after her mother and Noreen wrapped up for the night after the misunderstanding was revealed. She messaged one of the track girls to give her a brief correction.

HannahBanana: *Hey*

Abigal29: *How r u?? So sry again abt ur dad*

HannahBanana: *Yeah abt that..I think there was a lil confusion*

HannahBanana: *He didnt die overseas*

HannahBanana: *He was injured*

Abigal29: *Ummm....wow? So he's ok? lol*

HannahBanana: *He's back home*

HannahBanana: *It was complicated*

HannahBanana: *Helicoptered in from Syria to Europe*

HannahBanana: *That's why it took awhile*

Abigal29: *Ooookie. cool i guess. thts nice 4 u guyz*

Abigal29: *Well...i g2g*

Abigal29: *Nite*

[Abigal29 signs off chat]

That had been the extent of Hannah's retraction. The girls had been unkind in the ensuing days, since Abigail had spread the news snidely. Some snickered around her whenever she would walk into a room or through the field to prepare for practice. A few had muttered things like "wanna-be Orphan Annie" and "liar liar, terrorist pants on fire" which made her want to stick her head in a notebook and take deep breaths so she wouldn't cry.

At track that afternoon, her face didn't flush up like it had in the past few weeks. She ignored them and they ignored her. The coach didn't notice anything different. Today, however, the girls were giggling and looking in Hannah's direction.

"Did you know he was in the insane asylum at the hospital," one girl exaggeratedly whispered to the others. "No wonder she told people he was dead."

Hannah kept her gaze averted. She didn't know news of his treatment had spread. He had returned for one meeting with Dr. Finland and another specialist last weekend and someone probably recognized him. It was a small town, despite the bustling medical center. Things like this weren't easy to hide.

Also harder to hide was her flushed face.

"She told me three different versions of the story," Someone's voice chimed in, jeering in Hannah's direction. Hannah recognized it as Abigail, who had not been overly malicious before, but now that she had a juicy tale she was moving up in the social hierarchy at their school. "He was probably locked up for being mental all along. That story about Doctors Without Borders was all made up. She's just trying to get attention since her kind are all over the news." The snickering continued. "Newsflash! No one cares about raghead Muslims killing more raghead Muslims anyway."

Hannah was never confrontational, and she knew that the other girls knew it. Counting down the minutes to the end of practice and days until school was over, she picked at the grass.

Their coach blew into her whistle. The shrill sound broke the bullying and Hannah gratefully stood up and started her drills. Her emotions were in her throat. She was shocked that their teasing had turned into deliberately cruel comments. The drills were quick, and within a few minutes they began to run laps around the track.

"Hey," panted one of the girls, catching up from behind her. The others ran in unison ahead and a few looked back to smirk, noticing Hannah closing in.

Rebeckah wasn't in any of Hannah's classes, but they saw each other during lunch and in the hallway. She was friendly and smart. Her waist-length blonde hair was tied into a ponytail that swished back and forth lightly across her back as she paced herself with Hannah's momentum.

"Ignore them," she told Hannah, furtively looking ahead to make sure the other girls didn't notice her befriending their current target. "They'll find something else to talk about." She gave a half apologetic smile and sped up to join the rest.

Ignore them, Hannah thought to herself. How simple it was to just invert her emotions inside, fueling the already festering feelings that were boiling from her father's return home. The sun was slowly descending, yet still shone brightly against a brisk, blue sky. She focused on her breathing and steps.

She didn't feel like going home. The strangeness of her dad's behavior combined with her mother's obvious attempts to keep things light and optimistic was emotionally grueling. Everything seemed strained and fake. Noreen was busy with her friends and added activities at school. She had started to sneak her phone to dinner and would text under the table when Dahlia was busy trying to engage their dad in conversation. Occasionally, he stayed at the table and would inhale food as if he was famished and had been hungry for days. Other times he would nibble and look intently at the utensils and dishes, making minimal effort to join the forced conversation.

Hannah, upon Dahlia's pointed gaze, would offer a few comments at dinnertime, but soon made excuses about home-work. Instead of homework, though, she sat in her room and sketched. Stormy clouds, clouds heavy and still, and clouds atop tall mountain peaks. Her perfect family had crumbled and her drawings reflected it. They were hidden between her mattress and box spring so she could avoid a discussion pointing out the obvious. Her mom was overly in tune with things that reflected what they were feeling.

Yes, life was tumultuous right now. Yes, everyone should keep trying and be patient. Yes, her dad was home, but the more days that passed, the more it seemed like things may never be the same. She allowed her mother to discuss therapy techniques, drug side effects, and support groups, but she didn't respond or engage in conversation. What would be the point?

Her dad had set out on a three month journey to help people with his skills and he returned damaged and hurt, and hurting those who loved him. It wasn't a tangible hurt. She wasn't sure how to wrap her head around the devastation of not being able to turn to someone she always used to depend on. The few weeks at the hospital were hard, but since he wasn't home yet, it was still easy to avoid and assume he was just going to pop up on Skype like he had the first months he was away to chat about the people he had met in Syria. They all looked forward to those, not knowing the wholesomeness of his physical and mental states were soon to be mercilessly tossed in the wind.

A whistle shrieked again and Hannah leaped out of her thoughts. Her breathing was heavy and she welcomed the cool down exercises as the team finished their laps before heading back to the locker room to shower and dress. Her teammates avoided her and she avoided them. The girl who had spoken with her walked with Johanna, one of the outgoing girls on the team with a strong personality. Hannah recognized that they were aloof to the drama, but even knowing she had some silent backing didn't help when she felt so alone.

After her shower, she put her jeans back on and donned another long-sleeved shirt. Her white workout scarf was shoved in with her track clothes. Hannah ran her fingers through her damp hair, leveled it at her shoulders and tied it into a quick twist at the base of her neck. She wrapped an oblong scarf and left the ends loose, cascading down the front of her shirt.

It was time for prayer. Hannah and Noreen got comfortable with the concept of regular prayer at an early age. At home, they prayed together. In school and around town, they just found a corner and directed themselves on a small, folding prayer rug, taking a few minutes to reflect on their day when it was time, engaging in ritual prostrations and silently reciting Quranic verses. Regularly stopping at different segments during the day to reflect and perform prayer was beyond comprehension to a lot of people, but because of the conservative nature of Texan communities, they appreciated God-consciousness even if they found the visual of kneeling and prostrating strange.

Hannah found a spot near the end of the track field where there wasn't much foot traffic. She had prayed there since the start of school and barely anyone noticed. Once, a teacher spotted her and wanted her to speak during class about her experiences practicing a faith foreign to the average student, but she declined. Hannah wasn't interested in public speaking. Prayer was a part of her identity and talking about it to a group of strange students and a fascinated teacher was something Noreen would do better. With that in mind, she referred the teacher to Noreen and her sister was thrilled. Noreen had, backed by the approval of her very enthusiastic and amused parents, bought scarves and caps for everyone in the class. She even made them miniature prayer beads. After a quick information session about Islam and Muslims, she mimicked YouTube *hijab* tutorials for the sixth graders who collapsed in giggles looking at one another and used the beads as bracelets.

Reminiscing on her sister basking in being the center of attention, Hannah fiddled with her own bracelet. It was a gift from her dad, something he'd added to every birthday since she turned seven. Each year he added a new charm, and it was always something special, signifying a moment they shared that year. Hannah cherished it more than any piece of jewelry she'd ever had. Noreen would change jewelry at a moment's notice, often wearing different accessories at different times of the day, but Hannah's fashion sense, or lack thereof, didn't change.

"Hannah," shouted her coach, as she was going into the parking lot where Noreen waited in their mom's old car. The coach jogged in her direction with a clipboard held against her side. "Our next meet got changed to Friday afternoon instead of Saturday," she explained. "I didn't get a confirmation email from you noting the change. You've been lagging behind the past few weeks, but please kick yourself into gear!" She ended her request with a quick fist pump and gave her more details before rushing away. "Your sprints aren't epic enough to do much if your time is stagnant. I'll push you into long distance this time and see what you can do. Load up on carbs beforehand!" Hannah nodded and moved her duffel bag higher onto her shoulder.

After opening the backseat and dropping her backpack and track bag there, she slammed the door, venting some of her frustration at the verbal jabs she'd endured before practice.

Noreen was sitting in the car, texting furiously. "*Finally*," she said without looking up. Disdain dripped from each syllable. "First of all, don't slam my car doors. Secondly, hurry up next time. I was here for almost 10 minutes!"

"Relax," Hannah muttered to her sister. "It's not even your car. Did you pay for it?"

"Oh like you paid for your new track shoes?"

"You don't even like to run, why are you talking about my track shoes?"

"Can you do anything but sulk these days?" Noreen asked with scorn in her voice. Hannah knew her sullen face only aggravated Noreen further. She didn't have the kind of fake energy her sister did to pretend their problems weren't on their minds constantly.

Everything was going smoothly for Noreen at school and she spoke about all her different projects at home, when she wasn't texting on her phone. Hannah raked in their mom's sympathy at home, sometimes just curling up next to her as she did paperwork or going into their parents room on weekends to nap since their dad was using the guest room.

Upset again at the shaken dynamics of her once stable home, her anger flared. "Can you do anything but get on my nerves?" Hannah snapped back. "I had to pray after practice. You're usually late anyway so don't even try to blame me!"

"Jeez," breathed Noreen, rolling her eyes. Hannah kept quiet on the drive home, exasperated with Noreen and her constantly picking a fight. The only way she got to drive the car to school on a daily basis was if she promised to pick up Hannah after her track practice and run any random errands before going home. She made it really obvious that picking up her little sister from junior high was a super drag.

Hannah didn't care to sympathize.

Both sat stiffly in their seats. Hannah was looking forward to when she'd be able to drive herself home from practice. Her arms were crossed and jaw clenched, swallowing the jittery emotions. If things continued the way they were going during track practice, she would just skip the school altogether and drive away somewhere distant and peaceful.

The silence in the car was thick, but neither girl took the trouble to glance at the other. They were sitting in similar positions. Shoulders taut, eyes intense, and each nibbling on her bottom lip.

⋮

After Dahlia and the girls left for the day, an incessant ringing and knocking pulled Adam out of bed. His ankle was slightly sore as he hobbled down the stairs. The noise was making a muscle in his eyebrow twitch and he wanted it to stop immediately. His hair stood on end and his eyes were bleak. He had donned his old Beatles t-shirt and sweatpants after showering last night.

Or maybe he had showered yesterday morning.

It could have been the morning before that.

He couldn't remember.

After opening the door, Adam wished he had just crawled under the bedcovers instead, with a pillow over his ears..

Daniel was standing on the doorstep, grinning.

"There you are," Daniel exclaimed, deliberately ignoring Adam's scowling face and disheveled appearance.

Many of his colleagues had sent flowers and cards when he was in the hospital, wishing him a speedy recovery. Many more had visited because he had been a fresh and jovial face around the hospital campus, full of vibrant energy. They had missed him and were truly saddened when they heard about the catastrophic ordeal the Doctors Without Borders team experienced, especially when one of the team members was their prized Dr. Jamal. There was pity in their eyes when they saw him and after awhile, he requested no visitors.

Daniel wouldn't listen. He was a fellow ER doctor and also a new Muslim convert. After studying religion for years and filtering in and out of different faiths, he chose Islam just the year before and stuck with it with wholehearted determination, despite the turbulent issues it caused between him and his Southern Presbyterian family. Adam was excited at the prospect of another Muslim buddy, especially in the ER. Before his trip with Doctors Without Borders, he had even joked about playing matchmaker and helping Daniel find someone who shared similar values and knew how to grill a true Texas BBQ.

"I ran into our buddy Imam Hasan at the masjid," Daniel continued, referring to the imam who led regular prayers and gave sermons at their local mosque. "He said you were refusing to see visitors, but I thought to myself, who wouldn't want to see good old Imam Hasan?"

The rhetorical question hung in the air as Adam stared at both Daniel and Imam Hasan. The Imam was dressed in beige khaki pants and a blue button-down shirt. The striking white and gray in his hair, along with his long beard, reminded everyone who came close to him of Gandolf from Lord of the Rings. When he put on his long robes, or thobes as they were more popularly referred to for men, he could be a close second to the wizened wizard. There was currently no physical indicator that he was in a position of religious authority, but he was a man of great scholarly knowledge and wisdom. Their community loved him for his humility and gentle manners. He and his wife were significantly older and childless, but both managed to sweep the members of their *masjid* into a loving community family.

"*As Salamu Alaikum, Adam,*" the Imam greeted him, smiling.

Adam murmured a response, visibly uncomfortable and embarrassed, and turned away, already closing the door. "I'm tired right now," he began to say, in an effort to rid himself of the unexpected guests.

"No problem, buddy," Daniel stated. "I won't make you go out of your way to get us drinks and snacks like I would usually do. A few minutes will be fine to just catch up on how things are going. I know Imam Hasan has to rush to some meetings. Can we come in? Just for a few minutes?"

Adam paused, still fuzzy-headed and agitated at his inability to just wave them away. He silently consented and allowed the door to open fully, leading them from the foyer and down the long hallway where the den was.

Adam sat. Imam Hasan sat. Daniel stood, hands in his pockets, brows furrowing as he looked Adam over.

Adam noticed the staring and was more annoyed.

Imam Hasan had been wanting to visit Adam for weeks now. Dahlia kept mentioning his phone calls and the imam had tried to stop by before to see if a visit from a more spiritually centered person from the mosque might help him.

"God is so merciful, Adam." The Imam cut to the chase. He had counseled several people battling their personal demons in his many years in the Islamic clergy. "You were and are still a dynamic and spirited doctor." His gaze bore into Adam's eyes, imploring him to listen and digest. "You are so blessed to be home after experiencing the violence you did. It isn't about luck. But it is about God's will."

Guilt, anger, hurt, and betrayal soared into Adam's veins. God, he thought, suffocating in his desire to express his self-directed rage. How could he turn to God after becoming such a blatant failure. His temple started throbbing. The medications were doing more harm than good.

"Yes, I know," Adam replied. "The recovery is just slow. I'm tired."

"You seem more than tired, Adam. The light in your eyes, the conviction in your voice. There are more components at play with your mental health than just being tired."

Adam turned suspicious at his mention of mental health. "Are you saying I'm doing something wrong?"

"Wrong paths and right paths on the road to recovery are many, Adam. They can even overlap to expose new roads. It's natural to come back from a situation like yours with anger and sadness. It's important, however, to talk out your memories. To build on what you did accomplish there. Remember your team with love. I understand you've been refusing help from friends and coworkers, and even counseling. Prayers will always be a spiritual foundation of support, but being around others, especially those who are trained to help you, can be a crucial help."

Adam was struggling with deeper scars.

He almost felt crazy. He cracked some knuckles absentmindedly.

Doctors Without Borders was an exciting opportunity. He was in constant awe of his professors at the medical college who spoke of their experiences abroad, helping those in less stable countries. Never did he expect the instability his expertise thrived on would be his own downfall.

Suddenly, Adam's mind shifted into a different gear. He felt a million thoughts running through his mind at once.

He wondered if Dahlia set up this meeting.

Was she tired of him?

Tired of taking care of him?

Trying to get rid of him?

Was Daniel here only to make sure he was still too ill to work?

Did the Imam and God talk?

Were the whispers in his mind God?

Did the walls close in on everyone who survived Syria?

Or were they whispers, wanting to haunt him into senselessness.

He focused on the Imam's vivid green eyes, juggling the questions pummeling his mind, and nodded. "Thank you, Imam Hasan. Thank you, Daniel," he acknowledged in a hoarse voice, turning to his good friend. After clenching and unclenching his jaw for a few moments, he said, "I need to sleep now." He knew full well he wouldn't be able to sleep yet. Not with the static in his mind. "I'm on medication to keep me rested," he continued. "I'm trying to rest."

Rested was not what Adam felt. Daniel and the Imam glanced at each other. Adam hoped they would back off for now.

"Okay, buddy. We'll try to drop in and catch up some more later." Daniel reached out to shake Adam's hand, looking intently into haunted eyes.

"May God grant you a full recovery and put your heart and mind to rest," Imam Hasan raised his hands in supplication after standing and called upon God to shower blessings down from the Heavens.

Adam walked them back down his hallway, dotted with portraits and wall decorations carefully selected over their many years there. As Daniel and the Imam left, Adam closed the door with finality, relief flooding through his veins.

He turned to go back in the house and into the recesses of his gloom when his gaze passed by a picture Hannah had sketched of their family. Dahlia loved the realistic portrayal of the four of them and hung it up in the hallway immediately after ordering a colorful frame to accent the picture. Hannah's own self portrait, in particular, caused the shooting pain to start a twitch in his eyelid and the thunderous throbbing returned to pound inside his head.

A furry tail brushed at his toes and he jumped.

It was only the cat.

Zuzu silently observed him. Within his growing angst, he could feel the feline's judgement on him, too. Accusing and disappointed. Pain spread quickly and emanated now from every nerve in his neck, temple, and forehead. His t-shirt soon became covered with drops of sweat, trickling over his face and back. Overcome with discomfort and a budding nausea, Adam stumbled to the stairs and, being unable to stand on his legs, crawled upstairs and closed the door to his room, mercifully the first one along the row of bedrooms by the stairs. He leaned his head against the door and continued to breathe heavily, his complexion gray and pasty.

The ticking of his tableside clock magnified in Adam's ears.

He covered them with his hands, desperate.

Tick.

    Click.

Tick.

    Click.

Tick.

    Click.

Tick.

He needed to stop it.

Crawling again, he reached it.

Vomit bubbled in his throat.

Gagging, he swallowed it down.

Grabbed the clock.

The time on the clock was indecipherable.

Sweat poured down his forehead.

Into his eyes.

Adam couldn't tell if his tongue had swollen in size but it felt that way.

He felt helpless again, and that helplessness angered him.

Scared him.

Feeling that fear rise again, he shoved the clock to the floor.

It didn't help the ticking.

He reached out again.

There was a shatter.

The clock was broken. Shards of glass littered the base of his nightstand.

It set off itches in his brain.

Echoes.

Shattering windows.

    Shattering doors.

        Shattering bodies.

Death.

    He tried to focus.

        He tried to concentrate.

Grasped for the techniques he'd learned to fight the drop into his panicky memories.

    Breathing.

        Focusing.

Remembering. Remembering something hopeful.

Something that wasn't destroyed.

Adam traced his thoughts back to his homecoming.

The girls had strewn a banner together and put balloons in the front room on top of the fireplace. The fireplace was where they gathered for birthdays, anniversaries, and holidays. They would all leave presents on the brick hearth and glittered tile backdrop, and the first one to reach for a present had to make everyone hot chocolate. Dahlia insisted on trying new recipes, and they would all tease her about that one recipe gone awry when she had sprinkled in too much cayenne pepper.

It was Noreen, Adam recalled carefully, who tried to give him a mug of hot chocolate the day he came home. His wasn't clear on what happened after that.

His focus dipped.

The ticking in his ears returned.

Even though the clock was dead.

Just like all the bodies.

The clicking haunted him.

They haunted him.

The lack of clarity left a heavy feeling in the deep pit of his stomach.

Trying with all his strength, he remembered his clumsiness caused the mug to fall and the steaming liquid splashed over the cream-colored sofa he was sitting on.

Dahlia's favorite sofa.

Hot liquid. Splashing everywhere.

It was brown.

But the blood.

The blood splashes were red.

(78)

He was hopeless.

Helpless.

Exhausted.

He gave up.

The clock was a gift he'd opened on his homecoming day. His head moved away so he wouldn't have to look at it, broken, on the floor. He had teased the girls over Skype during his time in Syria that when he came home he wanted a huge party, balloons and presents included. He had missed them dearly.

The prescription bottles of pills were at his bedside table. He would sometimes take one on his own or allow Dahlia to remind him. The past two days, however, he'd hid the small pills under his tongue after giving the impression of swallowing them down with water.

Instead of ingesting them, he removed the pills from under his tongue and put them in the trash.

This new change signified his rebellion against being medicated. He didn't want to be drugged and helpless anymore. He wanted to feel, to suffer, to remember what time of day it was, to remember *what* day it was on his own.

He wanted control of his life again.

All of last night he had tossed and turned with the memories gaining vividness in his mind. What had been muddled before struck clear and worked to attack him from a million different angles. Finally, he crawled under the covers, dozed off as his throbbing temples pulsated him into oblivion.

⋮

8

Dahlia knocked on Adam's bedroom door. Hearing no response, she frowned. Her meeting with Dr. Finland hadn't gone well. He'd reacted with her progress report with growing concern.

"Well, I imagine we aren't understanding the full scope of his symptoms right now, Dahlia. He isn't communicating much, which is to be expected, but by now his sleep cycle should have provided him with some calm and ability to regain some of his usual routine. At least that should have given him the ability to begin reaching out instead of shutting down. You mentioned his speech seemed a little labored and faltering. Maybe it's time we look into other medications and even think about having him evaluated for a diagnosis beyond PTSD."

Dahlia blinked back tears when she heard the terms depression, panic disorder, and bipolar disorder. Dr. Finland did say the last was a long stretch, but it was better to be prepared for the possibility of a long term mental health diagnosis.

This wasn't supposed to be happening, she thought. He was supposed to be getting better, not worse.

Determined to crack through to her husband before he went through another round of drugs and evaluations, she knocked and called out to him. "Adam? Sweetheart, it's almost lunchtime. Are you up? I can make some sandwiches."

Deciding to ignore the closed door and no response, she twisted the knob and glanced around the room. Adam was lying in bed, curled up with a pillow over his head. The clock she and the girls had gifted him lay on the floor. A pristine, white blanket nestled around his lanky frame. The sore ankle was sticking out. She supposed he had reached to bring the clock closer and it fell off the nightstand.

Their present was face-down on the ground, small pieces of glass surrounding the circular instrument, its mechanical pieces sticking out in disarray.

Adam's body shifted and he grunted.

Accepting that as an invitation, Dahlia said *Salam* and started chatting about her day. There was nothing to fiddle around with or tidy up since Adam hadn't changed clothes for awhile and he wasn't doing anything in his room other than sleeping. She continued to give him a recap about anything that came to mind, sitting at the edge of his bed and looking down at the broken clock. Anecdotes, new patients, a joke she heard from the new doctor in her practice, and the girls different activities for spring filled the room with airy conversion.

"I keep telling my nurses that the girls are at each other's throats and they all say it's just part of the territory of raising sisters. I can't believe they're both teenagers now." She mused over how time had flown by. "I remember when they'd still roll around the sofas in their diapers and sing *Barney* songs."

No response from Adam.

Lips pursed, she moved her neck from side to side to work out the stressful kinks. "The plaza with the donut shop has a new tenant a couple of doors away. How many nail salons or massage parlors can they fit into each shopping center, do you think?"

No response again.

Frustrated, Dahlia poked Adam in the back. "I spoke with Dr. Finland today. He said he'll see you next week again to discuss your progress."

Adam shifted under his blanket even more, the pillow fitting snugly around his head, anchored with one arm. He grunted again.

Dahlia stared at her husband's curled up figure for a lengthy few seconds and sighed. She bent over and carefully inched the broken clock off the floor and shook it slightly, allowing the clinging fragments of glass to fall. It was so hard to stay bubbling with happiness and confidence. Every day that he had been home she wanted to shake him with joy and relief. She wanted to cry with tears of confusion, frustration, and helplessness. She couldn't do that with him, so she cried and talked silently to God in the heart of the night. She begged for patience and perseverance.

The day she and the girls brought him home was difficult. Hannah kept silent, and at any slight provocation she seemed to recede within herself on the sidelines. Noreen took cues more easily from Dahlia and tried to be upbeat and helpful as they drove home and welcomed him inside. After the hot chocolate spilled all over, Adam seemed rattled and Dahlia, not wanting to alarm him further, instinctively mopped up the mess with tissues from the end table. She didn't comment on the sofa but changed the subject. The dialogue was mostly carried on by her and Noreen. Hannah sat in the corner of the living room and followed directions but otherwise stayed quiet. Adam would murmur a response here and there. Dahlia knew there were medications in his system that were muddling his thought processes and despite not wanting to crowd him with incessant dialogue, she automatically resorted to that technique of calming her nerves and giving an aura of control over the situation.

Before she'd delivered Hannah, she had all the textbook knowledge of how babies came into the world gurgling and screaming. In addition, she'd already delivered Noreen, albeit completely drugged. She could dictate statistics, measurements, contractual pressures, and all sorts of nitty gritty information forwards, backwards, and sideways. When her labor pains increased, however, none of that helped. Thank goodness for Marlene. Hurricane season was upon them and it brought an onslaught of thunderous rain. During one such raging storm, Hannah decided to enter the world.

How contradictory it was, she mused, that her most calm and quiet daughter would be the one who would enter the world in the midst of such disorder and mayhem. Noreen was a chatter bug and Dahlia's labor with her came and ended quickly, unusual for a first baby. Adam was on call that evening and he slipped away to wrap Noreen's bawling, squirmy body in a hospital blanket and sing her a welcome into the world.

He was thrilled. She hoped to see that unbridled joy in his eyes again. If not soon, then someday.

Dahlia shook herself back to the present and tried to get a response out of Adam again. A few more pokes later, she gave up. Adam wasn't responding. She was sure he wasn't asleep, though, since he kept tightening the pillow over his head.

She tried one more time to engage him. "Sweetheart, did you want me to make you some tea? I know some of the medications could make you dizzy and queasy. I'm sure there's a stash of ginger or peppermint tea bags in the cupboards."

Not waiting for a response this time, she dumped the clock into the trash can with a loud thump. Frustration made her efforts feel forced, and her desolation sharpened. Leaving the room, she grabbed the handheld vacuum cleaner from the hallway linen closet and returned to swoop up the rest of the glass fragments.

Imam Hasan's wife had texted her earlier that her husband and Daniel had stopped in to chat. She had hoped that seeing his old friend and the Imam would perk him up and put him in a better mood. Apparently not.

She left the room, cradling the vacuum that had quickly cleaned up the broken clock. Time, like Adam, was slipping away from her. She closed the door behind her with a desolate, melancholy ache in her heart.

⋮

9

The 4th period bell rang, signaling the end of the class. Kids shuffled quickly from their desks and darted from the classroom. About half of them had lunch and the other half were headed to study hall. The teacher assigned to the study period didn't do much but surf the internet on her laptop and text. The students took that as cue to do the same, so most zoned out and either chatted between themselves or updated their social lives online.

Hannah and Abigail had 4th period together.

Thank God, Hannah thought to herself, that it was only one class. She couldn't imagine more time at school trying to internally deflect the teasing of track practice.

Abigail deliberately walked from her seat, crossing a row of desks, and bumped into Hannah's desk, knocking over a textbook and her pen. Hannah looked straight ahead until she saw Abigail leave the classroom from the corner of her eye. Then she leaned down and picked up her things, swung her messenger bag over her shoulder, and started out the door. Their teacher for that period was already writing notes for the following class.

Ashley, Hannah's only friend at the moment, waited in the doorway.

"Did that girl just knock your books over on purpose?"

"I don't know," Hannah sighed. "It's no big deal. She finally ran out of guys to flirt with in class, I guess. Plus, she was the one who thought my dad died and spread it around. When I told her he wasn't dead, she ran with that too, but not as nicely."

Ashley sympathized, but was agitated on Hannah's behalf. "That sucks. You can just tell her to shut up."

"I'll do that," Hannah rolled her eyes.

"You're taller than her. Just use intimidation. Knock *her* things off her desk. You're taller than most of the girls here, anyway. Be a mean giant!"

"You know me, just your average gentle giraffe," Hannah joked halfheartedly.

Ashley shook her head, annoyed with the bullying her friend was taking lying down. "Okay, I'll call you after school. Let's have some truffle talk time."

"Cool. I need that. Anything to get away from Noreen."

Ashley departed in the direction of the study hall. They were lucky to have been in each other's homerooms in previous years, but this year none of their classes matched up. The girls caught up in the hustle and bustle of the busy hallways between the 4th and 5th period bells.

Hannah was grateful for the few minutes of good vibes and a friendly distraction. She wasn't outgoing, and the few friends she had from grade school, she kept.

Abigail came from another elementary school that funneled into their larger middle school. Strangely, aside from track, they hadn't had any interactions before the misunderstanding about Hannah's dad. Noreen was actually friends with her older sister in some club or another.

Hannah sported a long zip up hoodie that day, with loose jeans. Her orange tie-dyed scarf was wrapped loosely around her head and tucked into the front of the well-worn top. She had her sketchbook in her bag and a Nutella sandwich tucked in for lunch. Instead of getting to the cafeteria before the 5th period bell rang, Hannah's eyes followed a group of kids who managed to escape the hallway scene by slipping out an emergency exit directly next to her.

Hannah paused, observing.

No bell rang. No alarm sounded in alert. No administrator barreled down from the office to shout about escaping students.

Impulsively, she followed the renegades and found herself on the other side.

Outdoors.

Soft air. Warmth. Sunshine. Cloudy wisps in the sky, nonchalant and comfortable in their ability to adorn such a vast expanse of beauty.

There was a calm outside. The chaos of the classrooms, students, teachers, and assignments were all, literally, behind her. Instantly.

The elation was short-lived, though, as her conscience kicked in. She turned around and started back into the building, but the door wouldn't budge. It was locked from the inside.

Hannah's stomach clenched as she glanced around, anxious to see if there were any other students who could clue her in on how to get back. The door had an emergency exit sign on the inside, so no one would be coming through it anytime soon.

"Hey, I didn't know you were the type to be *skulling*."

Johanna, the Jamaican girl from her track team, stood with her arms crossed against the far brick wall along their building. Her accent was thick and enchanting.

"Um, what?" Hannah asked, confused at both the term and encountering someone she knew on the other side.

"Oh right. You guys call it skipping school here. Playing hooky. Ditching. Cutting class. Is that more familiar?"

"No. I mean, yes. Yeah that's what it looks like I'm doing. But no, I'm not. I need to get back inside. I just saw some kids go out this door and followed. I'm supposed to be at lunch." Her words tripped over one another and she tried the door one more time.

"Girl, that's not going to unlock for another two hours. One of the tech club kids found out that there's an automated *unlock* at two o'clock, and the emergency alarm hasn't been hooked up since a thunder storm caused electrical damage. You're welcome for all the FYI stats, by the way.

Hannah remained confused.

Johanna began to saunter off. "In other words, you've got a couple of hours to kill. See-ya."

"Wait," Hannah cried out, following. "What are you going to do until two o'clock?" Not having any experience in ditching classes, Hannah was apprehensive. At least she knew Johanna from track even if they didn't have any classes together.

Johanna turned, hands at her sides. "What, are you serious? You just got out of school for two hours. Be free! The world is your oyster, as you Americans say." She tossed her dreads behind her head. Her shoulders were broad and her limbs muscular. It was obvious Johanna loved being active, and she exuded a confidence that Hannah didn't have. She also had an array of what probably was Jamaican jewelry on. A necklace, bulky earrings, and some bangles. Some flaunted a red, yellow, and green pattern, and they were all tied together by intricate black string-work.

"No, seriously. I need to get back in. I'll just go in through the front entrance then, if there's no other way."

Johanna groaned and covered her eyes with one hand. "Please. Please no. Don't turn yourself in." She sighed and lifted her hand, gazing at Hannah with pity and exasperation. "You'll be all honest and tell them about the door issues. That'll kill my daily mojo. Just use up your two hours today, okay? Then you never have to touch the door again."

Hannah shook her head. She was sure getting into trouble trying to be honest would be better than getting into trouble by being caught skipping classes. 2 o'clock was when the bell rang to signal the end of the lunch and study hall periods. Lunch was scheduled for half the school the first hour while the second half had study hall. Then they switched for the second hour. No one would be taking attendance during those times, but still. It seemed too disastrous to stay out.

Unless...

"Do you do this every day?" Hannah asked, curious and half-appalled.

"Yes, you crazy girl. Now come on. I'll show you your options."

Hannah dutifully followed. Her stride matched Johanna's, since both were tall. Johanna may actually have been taller than her, Hannah surmised. She couldn't wait to tell Ashley.

Ashely would inherently disapprove of Hannah's impulsive mistake, but she'd interrogate for every detail. With that in mind, Hannah kept a close eye on her surroundings, ready to give Ashley a full recap.

Johanna walked her down the side pathway and then towards the track field. Hannah kept looking back dubiously, sure that they were being watched and someone would come charging up to them, yelling accusations and threatening school expulsion. The sky was bright and there was a cozy feeling in the air. It was humid, but not as suffocating as the past few days.

Hannah's gaze returned to the school building again. Strangely, not many windows covered the back of the middle school building.

"That way," Johanna pointed to the far bleachers. "That's where you'd probably find the kids you followed out here. They like to hang out, smoke some weed, and either go back to class if they're not too wasted or just sleep it off until the buses come."

Hannah's eyes turned to saucers.

"Now that way," she pointed into a thicket of trees across the track field, is *not* where you want to be. Humid, damp, and full of mosquitos. Unless you're escaping school altogether and have a car picking you up on the road that runs on the other side, it's not too fun to mangle through."

Walking alongside a fenced ballpark area, Johanna continued in her nonchalant fashion. "If, for some reason, you have a pink slip handy that you've filled out yourself, you could manage to get picked up by some older kids with a car to go to the mall, get some lunch, whatever. Just act cool because you'll be within visible range of the front office windows if that's the case."

"What do *you* do," Hannah questioned, realizing she probably sounded like an idiot, but curiosity had taken over. She usually didn't delve much into people's lives at school.

Johanna dropped her bag and took off the sandals she was wearing. She then put on her track shoes and tied them tightly. Standing up tall, she addressed Hannah's question.

(90)

"I run. There's a trail that goes around the school and runs parallel to the boulevard, then circles back around the woods over on the other side of the building. There's even a small pond that has a bunch of ducks squawking around. Sitting around in classrooms all day makes me feel rusty. *Skulling* won't get me into trouble at home, even if I'm caught. Not sure about you, Ms. Good Girl. So think carefully. If anything, you can sit around here, have your lunch, and take a nap until two."

With that closing suggestion, Johanna sprinted away onto an unnoticed trail.

⋮

10

Dahlia stepped out of the maternity ward, relieved to be out of her scrubs. After delivering a set of twins, performing a series of circumcisions, and answering some anxious pregnancy questions through the clinic's emergency line, she just wanted to get home and stare at the wall.

Maybe that's an activity she and her now sullen husband could do together, she thought to herself, digging out her car keys from her overcoat pocket. Her sense of humor had gotten a little dark lately. Date nights were a laughable memory, meaningful conversation was at a standstill, and basic camaraderie was way out the window.

Marriage was a pretty grueling business solo.

The maternity ward had a side entrance that let out into a garden with a small trail that led to the staff parking lot. Dahlia paused against the door, looking back wondering if she had forgotten something. Oftentimes she and Adam caught a quick lunch together on one of the stone memorial benches. If he was tied up in the ER, Dahlia caught up on phone calls and emails while she waited.

"Dahlia," came a shout across the hall.

Glancing around intently, she caught sight of something so refreshing and delightful that heavy emotion choked her throat.

Marlene rushed to her friend and almost tackled her with a giant hug and bubbling laughter. "I couldn't wait to surprise you," she exclaimed as her curly red hair bounced with excitement in a high ponytail. She was also petite in height but nowhere near as dainty as Dahlia, with her vivacious personality and curvy figure. Where Dahlia was reserved and composed, Marlene's emotions were all over the place, along with her constant chatter.

The two friends hugged each other and laughed. A few people walked through the hallway and smiled at the obvious reunion.

"You should have told me you were coming!"

Marlene grinned. "I never do," she reminded her old friend. "At least this time my impromptu visit isn't timed around your delivery date."

Dahlia smiled at the reference. She had bags under her eyes and her face was pale. Marlene realized her suspicions had been right - her friend had a lot on her plate.

"Okay, let's go have lunch if you're free. If you're not free now, I'm here all week for a conference. Of course the only place they'll drag us out for a pediatric series on neurodevelopmental disorders is Booniville, Texas. The guys over in geriatrics got to fly over to San Francisco, so you'll be hearing me create a stink about this any chance I get."

Marlene chatted along as Dahlia soaked up her energy. The two women had met when they were both fresh into medical school and had synced into a great friendship. Marlene's ups and downs in the relationship department were also a source of amusement for Dahlia, who had hunkered down into marriage early on.

"How is Adam?" Marlene inquired, not wanting to beat around the bush.

"Okay. Not great. Not that okay either, actually."

"It can't be easy adjusting to normal life after experiencing something so gruesome."

"No," Dahlia accepted quietly. "But he's completely withdrawn. I feel like there's so much going on under the surface and I can't peek in at all. It's like living with a stranger who doesn't want to be there. They've got him on medication and he's not being responsive at all at home. It's already been a few weeks and...." She paused, choking back an eruption of the overwhelming feelings she kept buried.

Marlene understood her friend's abrupt pause. Dahlia had never been one to unleash her emotions, but simmering them inside couldn't be healthy either.

"Let's grab some coffee. You need to talk more than I do."

Gratefully, Dahlia consented.

"Why don't you come over if you're done for the day at your neuro-fun conference? I have some leftover cardamom from when Adam's family dropped in. Perfect for chai."

"Chai sounds like a treat. I will definitely take you up on this. But I think right now we should go somewhere else to clear your head," Marlene suggested, realizing that with Dahlia's personality, she probably hadn't given herself a break.

"Speaking of chai, you always make it sound so exotic." She added, playfully, "Have you found any cute Indian men at those huge family weddings you go to all the time? I wouldn't mind being served chai on a regular basis."

"For a firecracker like yourself, I'd suggest hauling over to India and scoping the scene to find yourself a true Bollywood hero."

"You know what humidity does to my hair," Marlene teased back. "Chai tea lattes at Starbucks it shall have to be then."

Dahlia pushed open the door.

"I forgot how thick the heat was here," Marlene commented. "I know I say that each and every time I visit, but seriously, how do you handle it? Especially with your extra coverage?" Marlene gestured dramatically at Dahlia's scarf and long-sleeved outfit. "I would be sweating up a storm and it would not," she finished emphatically, "be pretty."

Dahlia laughed. "You get used to it. Plus, my hair would become a frizzy, limp mess."

"My curls are frizz central for sure."

Warmed by her friends presence, Dahlia continued to smile gratefully. "How have you been doing, really? I can't believe you made it down here. I'm so glad!"

"It's been awesome. When did I see you and the girls last? Was it during Thanksgiving or was it early autumn?"

"It must have been way before Thanksgiving! But it doesn't seem that long with all our late-night texting sessions."

Marlene laughed, "How true." She added, "Oh! I think it's fabulous that the schools are letting kids out to run the trails during the day. I thought I saw Hannah as I drove in yesterday before our afternoon conference sessions. She looked like she was having a great time."

"What?" Dahlia countered, confused. "I'm sure the school doesn't allow that. Those trails go on for miles and head in all sorts of directions. It was probably someone else."

"Someone else wearing a scarf and running? How many Muslim female track athletes does this town have?"

"You'd be surprised. Before the weather gets horribly hot, everyone is outside."

"Horribly hot? So this is not so horribly hot?"

Dahlia laughed. "Yes, exactly. The mosque's recreational program committee plans a lot of outdoorsy activities. Hannah and Adam would go on hiking or biking excursions often." She paused to turn the car on and let it air out with the air conditioner blasting inside. "Noreen would go with him to plan youth group activities."

Marlene took that as her cue to start gently probing her friend.

"Have you and the girls taken him out to do something like that since he's been back?" she asked.

Dahlia fumbled with her purse. "No. He hasn't been himself at all. The girls haven't wanted to go either. I think people questioning them makes them feel under the spotlight. Adam's been completely closed off. Even with the girls. There must be more to what he's struggling with, something about the trauma he faced that he hasn't shared. I can't put my finger on it, but I know there's something clawing beneath the surface. If only he'd let us in."

The drive was smooth and quick. Dahlia decided a late lunch would be better than a coffee spot so the women found a Tex-Mex restaurant and settled into a booth. Quiet Mexican music played, and vibrantly decorated sombreros lined the walls.

After placing their orders, Marlene jumped into the thick of it.

"Okay, Dahlia. Real talk. What will you do now that he doesn't seem to be getting better? Was there a timeline that should have shown progress? What are the probabilities he'll stay this way... indefinitely? I'm sure the psychiatrist has suggested an evaluation or some further testing."

Dahlia's shoulders drooped. "I can't imagine this going on forever. It scares me to the bone. I want to avoid having him admitted for an evaluation because at least at home he's surrounded by what's familiar and loving. I don't think he would consent to be admitted easily anyway, and being an adult, no one can force it on him. He's avoiding friends, closed off from colleagues. He barely makes it down to have meals with us."

"The girls must be heartbroken. You must be heartbroken. He's your other half."

Cradling her head in her hands now, elbows angled on the tabletop, Dahlia nodded. "There's such a void with him being here and not being himself. When he would call or Skype from Syria, he was as happy as could be. That was his dream. We were both ecstatic that it came true."

Marlene murmured in sympathy. "Have you been speaking with anyone? Therapy?"

Dahlia moaned. "Don't even get me started on the T-word." Sighing, she explained, "I've dragged Adam to therapy and I've dragged the girls to family therapy. By now, I should have all the therapists we've consulted at the hospital on speed dial. It's so frustrating being the only one who wants to go to these things and forcing the rest to comply. They sit there and sulk. I pick their brains a lot at home, too."

"Think about trying someone on your own, without the burden of dragging them. You can't take care of anyone if you wind up getting burnt out. My cousin wound up in the psych ward because she bottled up some intense emotions and eventually snapped. No one is immune to breaking down, Dahlia. Not even you."

Touched by the heartfelt reprimand, Dahlia nodded. "I thought I could manage. In my head, Adam and I were still a team. There was a game plan in mind when he came back. We were so terrified after hearing the news of the attack and couldn't imagine a bigger blessing that him being flown home. Now, with this brick wall and no sign of real recovery or response for so many weeks, it's feeling like a bottomless, never-ending pit."

"There's a team of doctors who want to ensure he'll get better, Dahlia," Marlene reminded her. "Don't forget that. They'll also want to ensure you're doing as best you can under the circumstances. Why don't you take a leave of absence for awhile? Maybe stop the runaround schedule and trying to juggle everything?"

"It's routine," she responded. Their plates of food had arrived and both murmured their thanks to the waitress. Lifting a fork, she mused. "It helps to keep busy. I don't mind the hospital visits and deliveries. I would probably go just as crazy at home, if not more so. Adam would be heading that ship."

"Captain Cuckoo?"

"Sailing through the Loony Lagoon."

Both laughed, relieved to be able to joke about something difficult. "Tell me about the girls," Marlene promoted. "How's my namesake? I don't know how to pick a favorite. They're both so darling."

"She's such a sweetheart, and so sensitive. Taller now than when you last saw her. Still has her head in the clouds. Noreen has a tougher backbone and is always busy, but Hannah has been spending a lot of time alone, becoming quieter and more withdrawn. It hit them both hard, but she's visibly shaken. She and Adam were so passionate about her being on the track team. I'm glad she's still continuing it."

Marlene smiled. "She must be wearing her charm bracelet all the time."

"Never takes it off," Dahlia proclaimed proudly. "She's a creature of habit. Sentimental down to the bone. Noreen picks on her a lot, but given their ages, I guess there are a lot of hormones in the air."

"Any boyfriends?" Marlene teased.

Dahlia genuinely laughed. "Oh, goodness. I hope not. I think I scare them enough with all my childbirth talk that they balk whenever anyone mentions being in a relationship. Their dad's side was over not too long ago to check up on Adam and one of his older sisters kept commenting on the girls getting prepared to be married. Noreen was livid and Hannah just turned beet red and almost buried herself in her scarf."

They continued to talk about Dahlia's girls and slowly, and through laughter and the relief of finally expressing her true fears and hopes, the weight that had ensnared Dahlia's heart with its viselike grip loosened. Marlene's visit was just what the doctor ordered, and exactly the kind of deliverance she'd prayed to receive.

⋮

11

With her phone buzzing with text message alerts, Noreen woke up and shuffled through her bedsheets to find it. Once she got her hands on it she opened it up immediately and read multiple messages from different group chats. One was about the history exam coming up and a study group she and some girls had formed. Another rattled on about the international book club that was catching a little more attention because the advising teachers wanted to collaborate with cultural clubs. A few more single messages highlighted as she was scrolling through, and she clicked on the one that piqued her interest.

Keith: *Hey sleepyyyyyyy face hope ur up*

Keith: *Guess not..buzz kill. Can u help me out wit wrestling team interviews 2day after skl*

Keith: *How l8 do you sleep in on a skl day neway???*

Keith: *Does it take a long tyme to rap a scarf around ur head lol*

Keith: *Bfast is for winners. I know ur destined for greatness so dont skip the most imp meal*

Noreen hid a smile, even though she was alone in her room. She and Keith had been texting on and off. He mostly asked about grammar advice that he said he didn't want to bore himself with during the yearbook committee's weekly meetings. His teasing comments had started recently and she thought they were cute. He was dating Felicia, she surmised, since they were whispering together in the hallways and during yearbook committee meetings, so she knew he didn't mean to insinuate anything more than a friendship. Even so, she deleted the messages after replying just in case her mom browsed through her phone.

Noreen: *I may be up at the crack of dawn, sure, but not for long!*

Noreen: *Wearing a scarf just saves on time – no need to fix my hair*

Noreen: *g2g, no time for bfast! see you at YB mtng*

Her phone buzzed as soon as she dropped it, so she picked it up as she swung herself off the bed and fiddled around with different necklaces and bracelets on her dresser. Everything was organized first by color, then size. She loved the large expanse of dresser-top space to keep her fun, everyday accessories available. The fancier things were arranged in a closet organizer and hung next to coordinated outfits. Cardigans, dresses, scarves, pants, and everything was systematically sorted once a week when she did laundry, so she knew what to wear. The exciting part was to add in some flair each morning.

The loose tendrils of her curly hair fell over her forehead and into her eyes as she dropped one bracelet in exchange for another. She yawned a still-waking-up type of yawn, reading the message.

Keith: *Seeing you = highlight of my day ;-)*

Her fingers paused and she thought quickly about what to reply. There was no way she was going to get involved with a guy. Definitely not this kind of guy, flirty and cute or not. Being some dude's flavor of the week held no appeal. She had ambitions and goals and a to-do list that was a mile long and reached into the following five years, including LSAT preps and law school entry essays. Plus, she wasn't going to get into something with a guy at school only to have to hide it and live some undercover life. A lot of girls who had a more conservative religious upbringing fought against not being able to experiment and got involved in relationship after relationship, the urgency of keeping things secret only adding to the appeal. Not her. She saw what emotional chaos did to her friends and classmates over quick-to-fizzle romances, and worse, meaningless experimental hook ups that left them agonized. She sighed and flipped her thumbs over the keyboard quickly.

Noreen: *You've gotta find more hobbies dude*

She switched the screen on her phone off, took that day's outfit with the hanger, and headed into the bathroom. The guest room door was open and she sensed that her dad was awake. Awake didn't mean ready for a conversation. She paused and continued down the hall. Had his recovery made any progress, she would have poked her head in to at least give a cheerful good morning. As it was, his eyes were heavy with medication and sleeping issues. His temper was becoming more unpredictable. Last night at dinner, he rattled everyone by abruptly getting out of his chair so quickly that it fell over and leaving the table. This change in character was the worst. It was obvious none of them, especially not Hannah who remained nervous and tearful the rest of the night, knew how to maneuver around his rage.

In the shower she couldn't stop thinking about how she kept adding more things to her life to keep from acknowledging what she couldn't do at home. She wanted to succeed and find happiness somewhere, anywhere else. Her mother's attempts at keeping conversations light and festive only made her feel more pressured to do the same.

Hannah just shut down, Noreen reflected, annoyed. There was no help there. With her hair rinsed, she slipped out of the shower stall and got dressed quickly. Hannah was probably downstairs already because she was an early bird. So was her mom. That was one trait Noreen had zero guilt about not following.

She slid down the hallway and intended to slip right into her bedroom. She looked back and saw that her dad's door was still open. She paused, hovering at the doorway, and took a step inside, gently announcing her presence. She spent some evenings unable to sleep just reading about his diagnosis of PTSD and how the therapy he was refusing may help get him back into a normal groove quickly. Well into her teens, she was pretty confident about her abilities to research Web MD about the inner workings of almost any medical ailment. Being squeamish about blood made her turn away from her parents choice of careers though.

"Dad," she whispered. "Good morning." Noreen stepped into the room a little more. Adam was sitting at the edge of his bed, medicine in hand and the trash can tilted at his feet. He looked over blankly for a second and blinked in recognition. A flicker in his eyes made her feel agonizingly helpless. She pressed on. "I'm about to get ready for school. Do you want to go downstairs with me for breakfast?"

Whenever he didn't come downstairs, Dahlia brought a tray for him after the girls went to school. He slept so much and skipped meals so often. But for the past couple of days he seemed to be awake whenever she was around.

"No," he croaked. His morning voice was uneven. "Not now."

His gaze fell from hers. She pressed her hands into her stomach and tried to ease her sadness. "Okay," she whispered, not hiding the tears in her voice. The sudden surge of heartbreak was difficult to drown out. Her lips trembled and she pressed them together to gain some composure. It was rare that she found him alone, and the pressure of keeping her devastation concealed was crushing. He wasn't the father she remembered. Yet, his presence was a stark reminder of their relationship. Somewhere inside this sluggish, frail, broken, and harsh-voiced man was the man she loved and depended on with all her being. Her sweet father, with his exuberance for living and loving life, had drifted away somewhere inside the recesses of this person's mind.

Noreen took a breath, channeling in her mom's positive energy and proactiveness, and braved forward. She was halfway in the room when he finally noticed she was closer. His hand shook and all the pills fell from the medicine bottle. She looked at his face and realized his eyes were strikingly red.

They frightened her.

"I'll clean it," he roughly admonished her as she kneeled and swept some pills from the ground. Her hand trembled slightly and she dropped the pills.

"Okay," she said again, retracing her steps backwards and out of the room. She was quick to compose herself and dash downstairs. Hannah was drinking juice and wearing another boring outfit. Their mother was finishing up her coffee and looking through some papers with her laptop open. As she entered the breakfast nook, they both looked up.

"Good morning, sunshine," Dahlia said brightly.

"Finally," Hannah murmured.

Ignoring Hannah, Noreen chatted about the things she had planned today. She didn't bring up what had just happened upstairs with their dad. Dahlia was looking more refreshed since Marlene had come into town. They'd had lunch together two days in a row.

"Let's plan a dinner before your Marlene Auntie leaves," Dahlia suggested. "She'll finish up her conference soon. Maybe tonight would be good. I'll send her a text message."

The girls perked up and even smiled at each other for the first time in days. Marlene Auntie was super cool.

Later that afternoon, Noreen met Keith to interview some of the wrestling team. They were supposed to create a hashtag style page next to each team picture with the thoughts of team members from the year. Keith, being a football player, seemed to take great offense to the wrestling team and their so-called wussiness. Spandex-wearing nerds, he called them.

He called them worse names, but she ignored him.

Keith waited next to his locker with Felicia, who looked uncomfortable. He was playing with one of her series of earrings and she nodded to whatever he was murmuring. As Noreen pretended not to notice and skimmed through her phone, Felicia glanced up and awkwardly left the scene, her backpack clutched under one arm.

"Hey, there," Keith walked in her direction.

"Oh, hi," Noreen replied. Her bright red scarf was wrapped in a twist around her head and swept around her face and throat in a stylish way. No ear touching here, she thought to herself, not sure if it was a twinge of regret she felt or relief.

Noreen and Keith entered the gym, chatting about the upcoming football game. Noreen had never been to a game, and Keith was appalled. The wrestling team was seated on the bleachers in uniform when they approached. One of the members gave Keith a hard stare, and Keith glared back.

After asking some questions about their thoughts on wrestling and how it felt to play for their school, Noreen asked if they had any advice for freshmen and other students who wanted to try out for the team. The guy that Keith glared at spoke up. "Everyone gets an equal opportunity here," he said. His lips sneered in Keith's direction and elaborated "Some teams aren't as welcoming to people who look different."

Keith smirked. "Some teams," he said, "have standards to maintain."

"Oh?" responded the boy with a mockingly inquisitive voice. "Does this mean to play football in Texas you have to look a cookie cutter white boy?"

Noreen was surprised at their exchange and paused taking notes on her phone to look up between the two boys. She hadn't noticed any issues of racism at the school. Maybe the person attacking Keith had baggage because he didn't make the football team when they were having tryouts or something. Keith didn't give off any vibes of being judgmental, and Noreen didn't think delving into it further was going to help anyone out, especially because the tension was getting really thick. She cleared her throat and interrupted. "Well, thank you, everyone, for your thoughts! You'll see your comments with your team picture in the yearbook," she ended the meeting, smiling. The boy Keith had exchanged words with made eye contact. His deep brown eyes were piercing, as if trying to read her mind. He disconnected their gaze, swiftly leaping away from the bleachers and into the locker room, his wiry body aloof and commanding. The other members followed. It was obvious he was their unspoken leader.

Noreen and Keith walked out of the gym. She finished the notes on her phone. Keith turned to look at her and said, "What a crazy guy, right? He's always trying to pick a fight with me. Some people just want to get a rise out of others. I'm guessing he's grown up fighting and doesn't know how to communicate like normal people."

Not necessarily certain that was true since she had heard Keith make his own derogatory remarks, Noreen shrugged. She didn't notice his eyes look back towards the gym to make sure no one was following them. The hallways were clear after school, too. He lightly bumped her shoulder with his elbow. She looked up.

"Whoa. Am I in your way or something?" she joked, moving a few inches away.

Keith laughed, a dimple peeking from one cheek.

Of course he would have a dimple, Noreen thought. How cliche. High school football player. Charismatic. And dimples at no extra cost.

She laughed back, glad that some progress had been made on the yearbook tasks. Then she decided to end their meeting and get a move on. "Okay, I'm going to run. My sister has a track meet later today and I promised my mom I'd meet everyone there."

"Oh," he said, surprised. "I didn't know you had a sister."

"Yup," she replied. "She just started middle school, and our dad convinced her to try out for the track team. She's pretty good at it, if I understood all the hoopla right." Noreen rolled her eyes. "You know me and sports. I can't tell a football field from a baseball field."

"You're coming to the game tomorrow, right? You promised," he teased, reminding her.

"Umm...I'll try," she conceded. She thought convincing her mom would be easy since she was so overworked and distracted anyway.

"See you," he said, leaving her to exit from the side door. His arm deliberately brushed hers, though she chalked it up as an accident.

⋮

12

After Hannah met Johanna when she accidentally played hooky during school, a silent friendship had developed between the two track teammates. They even acknowledged each other between classes, stopping to exchange a few words about everyday things in the crowded hallways.

Once Johanna had sped off on the hidden trail, Hannah had tightened the shoelaces on her well-worn sneakers and done the same. Her messenger bag was safely tucked under one of the bushes that lined the ballpark fence. She'd felt elated, all her nervousness abating as the distance between her and school grew. She rounded the trail as it traced between thick trees, shallow ditches, and eventually, alongside a two lane road. A few cars had whizzed past, but Hannah didn't slow down. The small pond had crept up just as Johanna had promised, and Hannah took some time to enjoy the antics of the ducks. When she'd returned to school, it was almost time to go back inside. Looking closely, she could see a handful of kids alongside the bleachers, behind the track field, and even among the trees.

It seemed way too unreal that the teachers didn't know there were students milling around outside the school building in the middle of the day. Hannah felt a little unnerved that there was an entirely different world she wasn't aware of that wasn't contained in a classroom during school hours.

Not that she wanted to make a habit of leaving the building. Ever. But that one time had been exhilarating.

A shrill whistle signaled the girls to line up for their race. For long distance, Hannah always managed to make great time. In a one mile race, Hannah's speed picked up and steadily increased after the half mile mark. Her pre-game ritual consisted of clearing her head and getting ready to feel that rush of running, focusing on the sky. This afternoon there was hint of rain, so everyone wanted to hurry home before the downpour. Sprinters were on after the long distance runners, and hurdles would be set up soon after. There was usually another game going on in the middle of the track field, but not today. It was just their usual crowd of supporting parents, some coaches, and students.

"Hey, liar," a girl taunted cheerfully. Hannah ignored her. She had completely shut down at school and among her teammates, not counting Ashley and Johanna. Even at home she was rarely saying anything. Her mother was concerned, but with all the other obligations she was juggling, it was hard to draw Hannah out of her shell with the limited time they spent together at dinner.

"I don't understand why you're still picking on her," chimed Johanna from behind both girls. "Girlfriend didn't even say anything about her dad. It was *you all*," she emphasized with a pointed, accusing finger. "You were the one who made up all sorts of crazy things about her family. Enough is enough."

Johanna was their lead sprinter. She hated the relays and would pay any price to avoid marathons and was loud and clear about it. Their coach never argued with girls on what area they preferred, as long as they showed great times at the end.

Lindsay, the girl who was teasing Hannah, balked only slightly. No one wanted to ignite the wrath of Johanna. Rebeckah took a place next to Hannah. "She's right. Cut the crap. You guys started spreading it anyway."

Abigail, not as easily intimidated as Lindsay, sidled up next to her. She sneered at Rebeckah and Johannah. "Friends with the outcast terrorist now? Do you guys watch the news? Might want to be careful in case she decides to pack some explosives in that gym bag of hers."

Heat rushed into Hannah's cheeks and her eyes burned with quick, unshed tears. She had never been at the brunt of such vicious animosity before now. Especially for something that was so twisted and horrifying.

"*You* might want to be careful before *I* decide to explode your face in the pavement right now," Johanna retorted back, her temper visibly kindling.

Not at all bothered, Abigail lifted her chin and said haughtily, "This isn't your business so why don't you shut up, you Jamacian jungle rat."

"Jungles are preferable to looking like I belong in a neighborhood of pasty white trailer trash. You gonna marry your brother and go breeding in that bayou across town?"

"Guys! Stop it," Hannah yelled, jumping between the two sets of girls. Her instinct was to close herself off from saying anything and hide in the sidelines. Instead, she directed her temper to Abigail and Lindsey.

"My life is none of your business! Do you think your comments mean anything to me? You're absolutely *nothing* to me. You matter less to me than a pile of trash! Good luck having a meaningful life if you're going to be such nasty witches to people who don't even care about your existence! Abigail, your dad isn't even in your life, but you don't hear anyone of us picking on you about it. The man left you before you were even in school! Lindsey, your brother was arrested for drunk driving - should I go ahead and keep calling you an alcoholic now? Get a grip on yourselves. Grow up! Get away!"

Her furious tirade left her feeling elated and queasy at the same time.

Lindsay and Abigail huffed off after giving hateful stares and muttering more vulgar things. Johannah was laughing too hard at their expressions to respond. She caught Hannah's shell-shocked glance and finally managed to say between the rowdy guffaws, "Well, that was worth the wait."

Rebeckah and Johannah high fived, not able to stop chuckling.

Hannah blinked a few times, looking around and seeing that more girls had witnessed their argument and were awkwardly lingering at a distance. A couple of them gave apologetic smiles to Hannah. She wasn't about to extend any olive branches if that's what they were angling for.

"I didn't want you guys to get too crazy. It wasn't heading to a good place. You know, trashy rats and all that."

"You have enough crazy in you for all of us, Hannah," Rebeckah said. "I mean that in the best way possible. That temper was pretty legit. Didn't know you had it in you."

"Well," Hannah said, smoothing out her track shirt nervously. "I do have an older sister."

"Mmm...that'll do it." Rebeckah was grinning ear to ear.

Johannah was also ecstatic and jumped in. "Don't start feeling bad that you ran them up a wall. They're disgusting bullies. Nasty witches, like you said. The only reason I got mad was that you kept taking life lying down! It was obvious you weren't going to speak up for yourself, so someone had to. It just isn't right to let people treat you like crap whenever they want." She grasped Hannah by the shoulders and shook her a little. "I get that whole sticks and stones BS, but it's better to get things out and stop the madness when it's hurling itself at you. Time to run with your wake-up call and keep taking a stand! You did great!" She commended Hannah, proud and encouraging.

A shrill whistle signaled everyone to clear the lanes. Rebeckah nudged Johanna and asked, "Do you mind stopping the madness of that whistle while you're being all she-warrior?"

Johanna burst out laughing. "I just might have to do that," she agreed. "Unless Hannah wants to give it a shot," she teased.

Hannah shook her head, smiling, and lined up next to the other girls. Relief flooded her veins so tangibly she could have cried. She could never have imagined having an outburst and standing up against their comments, but it was worth it. She did feel bad though, she thought, reflecting. It wasn't fair of them to use her as a verbal assault target, but she definitely wasn't going to poke fun at people for situations not in their control. People had problems in their personal lives. It was a sad reality.

She quickly glanced over her shoulders as she leaned in line to see if her parents and Noreen had made it. The bleachers held a smattering of the usual parents, but no one in headscarves or the shadowy face of her dad. Dahlia had told her in the morning that it would be a great way for him to get some fresh air and see Hannah in action. That was her plan at breakfast, anyway. At the blast of the horn, Hannah and the runners leaped into action. Soon, nothing was on her mind except her feet eating up distance on the ground and the breeze that tickled her face.

Her heart pumped vigorously, in sync with each step. She was pounding away at the surface and soon reached a level of euphoria that filled her body with just the air going through her lungs and her mind tingling with heightened awareness. She remembered when she and her dad would go running in the early mornings and talk about a runner's high. He would explain all about the endorphins and nuances of how the feel-good happened when you reached a certain sweet spot in exerting energy for a long distance. She didn't care about the details, but loved spending the brisk daybreak hours together.

Hannah finished her long distance run in record time. She was still elated. Having someone speak up on her behalf made her feel silly for letting people get under her skin to such a degree. And lashing out at Abigail and Lindsey rattled her out of the cocoon she had created for herself. Knowing Johannah and Rebeckah were on her side and so thrilled for her when she did finally speak up for herself made her feel equally great. She looked around at the crowd of parents and families again and didn't see anyone to share the moment with. Shaking her head, she grabbed a water bottle and sat down on the bleachers to wait out their arrival, watching other teams do more track and field competitions. Thunder rumbled distantly.

She waited in vain until the last track race finished. A lingering Rebeckah kept her company since her mom was also late.

"Oh, finally," Rebeckah said, noticing a gray minivan pull into the track and field parking lot. "She's here. I'm glad it didn't start raining."

"Yeah," Hannah responded, looking at the darkening sky.

"Can we give you a ride home? You can't live that far."

"I don't, actually. Sometimes I get a ride home with one of my mom's friends, but she and her daughter aren't here today."

"Do you have a cell phone yet?" Rebeckah asked as they walked across the field towards the waiting minivan.

"Nope," Hannah said. "My parents finally got one for my sister when she started driving, and she's like so addicted to it now. I'm guessing I'll get one after I pass my driver's exam, too."

"I have four older sisters and they all got their cell phones before high school. Of course, now my parents are like, 'Oh, what's the point of getting you one since you can just use one of theirs?' Like that's ever happening."

"My sister would have her claws out real quick if I touched her cell phone," Hannah said, rolling her eyes. It was cool to finally have someone to exchange stories with who understood what it was like to have a crazy older sister.

Thank goodness she only had one, she thought to herself.

Living near a popular bakery helped navigate anyone to her address. Rebeckah's mom didn't mind dropping her off. Each extra minute Hannah had waited, hoping to catch glimpse of any of the three people in her family, had increased her exasperation. The exasperation grew into frustration, and by the time she buckled herself into Rebeckah's minivan, she was hurt, tired, and fed up.

She dutifully sent a text message to her mom's number through Rebeckah's mom's phone that the track meet had finished and she was getting dropped off.

As a bolt of lightning streaked the sky, she watched it mirror against her charm bracelet, causing it to sparkle for a split second.

⋮

13

Dahlia loaded one last carton box into her black suburban and closed the trunk. She circled to the driver's door and got in, her pastel pink scarf accenting her white coat. She had locked up for the day at the maternity clinic much later than planned. Adam wasn't responding to her phone calls home, and she wanted to make it to Hannah's track meet in time to see her race. Marlene was excited to join them for dinner, so there was also a quick trip to the grocery store she needed to squeeze in. Trying to juggle all the details in her mind, she took a deep, calming breath. Marlene's visit had reminded her to take some moments and destress.

She plugged in the key and turned the ignition. Nothing happened. She tried again and it was the same. She quickly became flustered.

"No way," she muttered, shaking her head. "Not this. Not *now*." Dahlia pounded her first at the wheel and growled under her breath. So much for calm breathing techniques. Adam's behavior was giving her a lot of anxiety. He refused to go to his last group therapy meeting, she had remembered during lunch with Marlene. All she caught from his grumbling was "annoying" and "too much punch."

Her shoulders were sore from doing paperwork the entire day. The steady stream of patients had come and gone with fairly normal concerns. Another doctor was on call at the hospital, and there was news of a couple of healthy and smooth deliveries, which made them all happy. The nurses were, as always, a Godsend. Her partners graciously filled in for her, but she felt guilty about the added work they were doing and tried to do additional paperwork and other administrative duties she could take home so she could keep an eye on Adam.

She was overworked, tired, and felt at her wits end. *Deep calming breaths my foot*, she thought to herself.

Picking up her cell phone, she dialed Noreen.

Probably because she had been on the phone texting, Noreen picked up immediately. *"As Salamu Alaikum*, Mom. What's up? Are we going to Hannah's meet? We'll be late if we don't leave soon. Not that I mind. I have to change, anyway."

"Walaikum As Salam, Noori," she said as soon as Noreen gave her a second to speak. Noreen was dependable and upbeat, despite butting heads with Hannah so much. Dahlia reminded herself to give her more credit for being so mature about her dad's illness. "My car isn't starting and I'm right outside the clinic. Could you swing by and we can go to the meet from here?"

"Sure," agreed Noreen. "I just got home. Like literally ten seconds ago." Dahlia heard a few things land against the floor. "I'm going to grab some library books from the study and return them since we're headed in that direction. Should I ask dad if he wants to go? I think he's asleep, though, because I rang the doorbell first and didn't hear him."

"Let him rest," Dahlia told her. He hadn't been sleeping well, if at all, the past few days. That reminded her that she needed to call and speak to Dr. Finland about moving up his appointment and seeing if there was a new combination of medications he could try. Maybe Dr. Finland could even convince Adam to attend group therapy again before taking more serious steps.

"Okay," agreed Noreen. "I'll be there in about fifteen minutes."

Dahlia hung up as soon as Noreen did. She saw one of the maintenance men pull up to the professional building and got out of her car. Oh, great timing, she said to herself with relief. Waving, she opened the door and stepped out. "Hello there," she called out. He waved back. "Do you have jumper cables? My car won't start."

The maintenance man tipped his wide brimmed hat in her direction. "No ma'am, I don't. What I can do is call my buddy Lloyd and he should have some on him. Sit tight."

Dahlia returned to her car after giving her thanks. After spending a few years in New York City, where people tended to growl at you instead of politely responding, she was so glad they had settled down South so her kids could grow up in a friendlier environment.

Noreen and the maintenance man's friend Lloyd both arrived at the same time. The men decided to jump her car while she waited inside the other car with Noreen, who caught her up on all the things she was doing at school. Dahlia tried really hard to concentrate and make supportive comments, but the jumping was taking longer than she'd expected and she was getting increasingly worried about making it to Hannah's meet.

"So, this girl Felicia has a brother in the psych ward?" questioned Dahlia, picking up on the tidbit from Noreen's breakdown of everyone on the yearbook committee.

"She said it was her twin brother. We've seen them from time to time. Not her brother, but she's usually with her parents going in or out."

"Isn't it strange how hospitals create a little family within themselves? That's why the group therapy sessions are so important." Dahlia added the plug in, hoping it would take root with Noreen.

Noreen groaned. "Mom, please. People socialize enough without scripted questions and awkwardness. If you wanted to get someone really treated for social awkwardness, I'm all for you and Hannah going on your own."

"Noreen," Dahlia responded, sternly. "That's enough picking on your sister, please. She's still very young..."

"She's not a child, Mom," Noreen interrupted, exclaiming passionately. "If you keep her inside a bubble, she'll never be able to function in real life."

"I think our life has gotten real enough, and she's dealing with it as best she can." That was the only mention either of them had made about Adam's plight. There was definitely an elephant in the car with a capital E, harnessed and unflinching, waiting for someone's acknowledgement.

Noreen didn't have a response.

"You have different personalities, Noreen. It's unnatural to expect her to cope the way you are. You're also older."

Noreen rolled her eyes. "Okay, fine. Forget it. I know you'll be leaping to her defense for the rest of my life." Surprised at the frustration in Noreen's voice, Dahlia inquired more. "Do you feel like you're not getting fair treatment at home? Have we raised one of you with some kind of favoritism?"

"Mom," sighed Noreen. "Don't get all therapist on me, please. I just don't think it's fair to expect me to treat her the way you do.

She isn't *my* kid. You can coddle her while she's wallowing, but I'm going to give her a reality check when I need to."

Not sure how to dig into the conversation further without adding more agitation, Dahlia stayed quiet.

"Did you have lunch with Marlene Auntie again?" Noreen was obviously changing the subject to more pleasant topics. Marlene was someone whom they all enjoyed thoroughly. Even Adam developed a soft spot for her after she delivered Hannah.

"Yes," Dahlia smiled. "She misses you. I still think we can manage to make a quick dinner if the car situation hurries up."

"No boxed spices?"

"Not tonight," she promised. "Maybe some salmon with veggies and your quinoa salad. Oh hey," she suddenly exclaimed, noticing she had Noreen's full attention. "Where's your cell phone?"

"I dropped it at home when I was upstairs changing and realized it when I got here."

Dahlia laughed. "Poor you. It must be like missing a limb."

"Now that you mention it, can I see your phone?"

The maintenance man walked over and Dahlia quickly stepped out, hopeful that something had clicked with the engine. Instead of good news, he explained that Lloyd had gone back to the maintenance office to grab something. "Sit tight, ma'am," he requested.

So she sat back in the car and cast her anxious eyes skyward. *I wonder if Adam ate lunch*, she thought to herself. Unconsciously, she gnawed at her lower lip. If he was taking his medications, he should be getting enough rest. *Unless*, she speculated, *he wasn't*.

The suspicion dug into her mind and she turned to Noreen, who was browsing the internet on her phone.

"Have you seen your dad take his medication? Does he swallow the pills when you're around?"

The abrupt question threw Noreen off. "Umm," she started to say. "I guess so?"

"Yes or no?" pushed Dahlia. "Have you seen pills enter his mouth and him swallow them completely?"

"Mom, I'm not watching his every move, okay? I went into his room this morning and he was holding his medicine bottle and dropped it. Maybe I spooked him. He looked really out of it, though. It was kind of scary."

Dahlia thought it must have been heartbreaking for her daughter, along with scary. At least Noreen could handle it. Hannah would have melted down.

"You know," she began. "Dr. Finland did want to see him for an evaluation. I'm not sure what's going on, but something isn't settling down right with your dad. Maybe something else can help."

"How long until he gets better?"

Dahlia looked at her hands instead of answering the question. Her nails were neatly cut and her hands seemed small. She knew they'd cupped an ocean-full of tears these past few months.

"Mom," Noreen prompted. Looking up, Dahlia saw her brows furrowed with tension.

"It may not be as soon as we thought, Noori. His progress isn't looking good so far."

After almost an hour of fiddling around, the maintenance men chalked up her car trouble to rusty cables and sprayed all sorts of toxic-smelling liquid around the engine. Soon after, her car was ready to go.

"I know I should have just gone ahead with you, but we probably need two cars for the rest of the weekend," Dahlia explained, half apologizing for the delay.

Noreen shrugged, watching her mother grab her work bag. She wasn't as chatty as she had first been when her mom got into the car with her. "You can tell Hannah all about it. She sent a text message from someone's phone to yours saying she was getting a ride with some Rebeckah and her mom. The meet ended." Noreen handed her mom's phone back to her.

Dahlia groaned. "I knew we were cutting it close. How mad do you think she'll be?"

"Oh, Hannah? She'll get over it," Noreen commented. "Maybe she didn't even notice."

"Well, I'm disappointed," emphasized Dahlia. "I was looking forward to watching her run. Let's try to make it up to her somehow."

Noreen didn't reply.

Dahlia shut the door of Noreen's car and walked over to hers, engine finally on and running smoothly. Thunder and lightning had crept up over them and a storm was quickly moving in. She slid into the driver's seat and signaled to Noreen to go ahead first. The entire way, following Noreen, she mulled over how to make it up to Hannah.

.

14

Hannah waved at Rebeckah and her mom as she let herself inside her own house. The clouds were turning dark, and a few drops of rain splattered on the sidewalk. She noticed neither Noreen's car nor her mom's were in the driveway. She threw down her duffel bag and slammed the door, still annoyed that no one had shown up at her meet. As she went into the kitchen, fuming a little more with each step, she tripped over Zuzu's cat toys.

She kicked the toys against the wall and continued back towards the kitchen. Thunder rumbled. Another quick, loud storm was headed at them. It fit her mood perfectly.

Hannah opened the fridge and slammed it shut, not looking inside. Then she grabbed an apple from the fruit basket and proceeded to slice and peel it with a knife. In her angst, her hand slipped and she sliced the webbing between her thumb and first finger. Blood dripped onto the fruit and the floor.

Hannah kicked the kitchen cabinet and began to cry. She smeared some blood over her face trying to wipe the tears.

Adam entered the kitchen, the small collisions Hannah had made being amplified in his mind. Every movement bounced loudly in his ears. He was removed from the present situation and his mind flashed back to the last moments he remembered in the small Syrian clinic.

"Dr. Jamal, all medical staff have been advised to leave the premises immediately. Rebel troops are making their way through our side of town and shooting anyone in their sight," a nurse advised, her brows raised in apprehension. She was a solidly built woman with strong shoulders and arms. Her energy level never ceased to amaze the rest of the staff. Her gaze was sharp as she reminded the doctor of their instructions.

Adam shook his head and continued to stitch a young girl up. "We can't just leave. There are kids here. Tell the guards to secure the doors and round up whoever we can move upstairs. Schools and medical camps are suppose to be off limits."

The danger had gotten very real within the past week. For most of his two and a half months in Syria, Adam worked in relative ease. He was an efficient and outgoing ER doctor in Texas. His reputation for dealing with emergency room situations spread far and wide. He published an array of articles in medical journals, which bolstered his reputation. A team of doctors from a different university town had requested he come with their team to join the group from Doctors Without Borders. He and Dahlia discussed the opportunity in length and both were excited at the chance to make one of his lingering dreams come true. It was only for three months, and the girls would be busy at school. They could easily talk over Skype, and everyone was sure the months would fly past in no time. The hospital even added someone else to the staff to help cover his shifts while he was away.

A loud explosion was heard from a distance. The girl he was working on began to cry. She reminded him so much of Hannah. Gangly, all elbows and knees. A shy face and whimsical gaze. She had been brought in with a large group of school children who got caught in an artillery bombardment between freedom fighters and government troops. Her injury was minor enough compared to the others he'd treated that day, and he used the sparse array of instruments he had to make quick work of the gash on her forehead.

The explosions got closer.

"Dr. Jamal," repeated the nurse, raising her voice slightly. Like him, she wasn't a native Arabic speaker. One of the doctors in their group was, and they used him to communicate with staff and patients at the clinic.

"Where's Dr. Omar?" Adam asked. The nurse scurried away looking for him. Adam smiled at the little girl and used his broken language skills to assure her she was fine. He nodded and said, "Safe, you are safe."

She looked worried because of the noise outside. Her head was wrapped in a scarf and he still couldn't shake the uncanny similarities between her and his Hannah at home. He hoped that her parents would know where to find her once it became stable enough to go outside. God, he hoped, must be at least that merciful.

"Do you like playing? Ball? Football?" Adam questioned, trying to distract her. He pantomimed kicking a soccer ball, knowing the reference would be clear. The American label soccer didn't work here, he'd realized much earlier on during his trip.

She quickly smiled, amused at Adam's exaggerated antics. "Yes," she responded in Arabic. "I play football."

The nurse was gone for several minutes. Adam removed his gloves and went looking for her. The doorway leading into the courtyard was wide open. He peered through to see what was going on. Several yards away, the guards were signaling to one another, and the nurse was frantically conveying to Dr. Omar that they needed to leave.

Suddenly, shots rang out and everyone in the courtyard dashed frantically in different directions. Men in heavy dark clothing swarmed in like adult-sized black beetles. They shot down the guards who had tried to fire back. Shock froze some of them for a split second, then adrenaline-driven panic kicked in. Adam rushed a stream of people inside before shutting and bolting the doors. Gunfire pierced the air.

The fighting wasn't supposed to reach their rural area. He and a few more staff members tried to usher patients upstairs. Someone tripped and fell flat on the stone stairs, and the delay caused shouting in their midst. A good number of patients were unable to move quickly. Adam hurried to grab two frail women who were lying on cots closer to the door - one under each arm - and took them inside the tiny operating room where he had just finished stitching up the Hannah look-alike. He glanced at her as she trembled with fear, eyes wide and worried, and before he could say a word something blasted directly outside their building. It might have been some kind of grenade to break down the bolted door.

More gunfire blistered their ears and women and children screamed. Adam approached the main area again. The door was kicked open, the bolt completely destroyed now, and several men entered the clinic. The nurse was being dragged back inside by her neck. Suddenly, she was thrown against the wall and pumped with bullets. Adam saw her body slump down to the floor, blood covering the wall behind her.

At home in the kitchen, Hannah screamed, startled and scared when her father grabbed her. She didn't hear him come downstairs. His grip was bruising and when she looked up at his face, he was wide-eyed with heated emotion. He started shaking her and dragging her a few feet from the counter where she had dropped her knife and apple.

"Dad," she choked, her face still wet with blood and tears. Her stinging hand was forgotten and real fear crept into her limbs.

Adam noticed the blood on her face and shouted,

Are you hurt?
ARE YOU HURT?

His voice was loud in her ears and he was inches from her face, breathing heavy. He yelled at her again,

WHERE DID THEY SHOOT YOU, HANNAH?

Hannah scrabbled to get away from him and screamed at him to let go. He struggled to hold her in place and she began to fight at him, clawing to get away. Thunder rumbled menacingly outside and lighting flickered sharply. Adam kept yelling, his eyes bloodshot and his grip on Hannah too tight for her to escape.

STAY HERE, HANNAH. STAY!
THEY WON'T TAKE YOU!
I WON'T LET THEM TAKE YOU

One of the armed men shouted towards Adam. They tried to shoot at him, but missed when he ducked away behind a wooden desk. One man, furious that Adam hadn't been struck dead, ran and jumped atop the desk, then shoved him onto the floor. He began kicking Adam, who felt his ribs crack under the barrage. Several other men continued to shoot anyone nearby.

The girl on the small bed screamed. The man looked up at the noise and entered the small operating room, forgetting about Adam writhing on the floor. He strode in quickly and grabbed her head in his burly hand. He shouted outside and two other men appeared.

Hannah managed to break one arm away from her dad and twisted her entire body, kicking at his legs. He wasn't letting go. She was screaming and sobbing as he continued to shout at her, too.

NO HANNAH!

NO!

WHERE ARE YOU HIT?

There was little light in the kitchen, and heavy rain pelting the home muffled their struggle. He tried to drag her from the kitchen, his mind focused on saving her from the demons his subconscious had spilled over into reality.

The two men in the small operating room grabbed the girl. Adam shouted in protest, having gotten up and heaved himself against the doorway. His frame was bent with the pain of the broken ribs, but his mind was on the girl. The same man who had pushed him onto the floor and kicked him swung his gun back from the other two women in the room. The girl screamed and fought against the men, who lifted her off the bed and began to drag her by her arms.

Gunshots were fired directly behind Adam, over his shoulder and into the two government fighters. The girl collapsed along with them on the grimy floor. Then Adam ducked. Another doctor at the clinic had been upstairs when the soldiers came in, and now he raced down the staircase after ushering patients into bedrooms upstairs. He shot at anyone he saw wearing camo, glasses askew over his nose and determination keeping his rifle steady.

The man who had kicked Adam ducked when Adam did. His brawny arms reached across the floor in a quick army crawl and he took Adam's head and began to smash it against the floor. Adam's ears were ringing and blood gushed out of his nose and mouth. He choked and struggled to wrestle him back and away. The soldier saw the women cowering on the floor trying to get away and grabbed his own rifle

Another soldier stormed into the room and shot the doctor who had killed two of his comrades. He fell to the floor, glasses falling off his face and shattering under the crushing weight of his lifeless body.

Adam reached out and grabbed the girl's ankle as the first man jumped up and began to drag her out of the room with him. Her lanky frame was easy for him to carry, but Adam's pulling at her ankle succeeded in making him furious. He kicked Adam again. The shouting from beyond the room had died under the roar of more artillery.

The girl screamed and struggled to get away. Adam was a bloody mess on the floor. The soldier aimed to fire at the doctor in a final attempt to punish and eliminate him. The girl swung out her arm and hit his rifle hard enough to unsteady it as he fired. The shot missed. He threw her onto the floor and clobbered her head violently with the butt of his gun, knocking her unconscious.

Adam was still trying to cling to her ankle and keep her back, away from further danger. The men were being called back from beyond the clinic and the remaining man holding the girl dropped her body quickly and rushed out, his heavy boots plodding over dead and bloodied bodies. The three other men fired their guns into everyone in the room as they rushed out. Adam slumped over with bleeding wounds, still on the floor of the operating room. The girl and two women were left for dead. The girl moaned, blood spilling from the cut Adam had stitched up not five minutes prior. It felt like five lifetimes ago. Adam could feel his body give up and his vision dizzied. He tried to focus on the girl, to soothe her somehow, but he was quickly succumbing to his injuries. Before his eyelids finally closed into oblivion, the heavy booted man returned and dragged the mirror image of his Hannah out of the room by her arm.

Hannah finally broke free of her dad as she slipped one arm out of his deathly grip and reached blindly behind her. A vase fell and glass shattered. Adam's body rocked as if he had been shot. Hannah ran out of the kitchen and into the den. Her father, breathing heavily, labored after her, his footsteps loud and menacing. She stumbled up the stairs and didn't dare look back. Lightning flashed as her father continued up behind her, still shouting incoherent questions and frightening promises.

Zuzu streaked through the hallway into Noreen's room and Hannah quickly followed. Noreen's phone lay on the bed, just a few feet from the closet. Hannah clawed at it as lightning streaked through the sky. Rain and thunder continued to pour onto their house as Zuzu slipped into Noreen's open closet. As another grumble of thunder orchestrated fury in the sky, Adam threw the guest bedroom door open, searching for Hannah.

Hannah quickly slipped inside Noreen's closet and her hands fumbled as she tried to twist the knob shut silently behind her. Her body was shaking as she crouched on the floor in the dark. Adam was shouting her name and she could hear things being thrown brutally around the adjacent rooms. She crept alongside the wall of the closet, Zuzu curling into her side.

With trembling fingers that could barely function, Hannah turned the phone screen on. Noreen had left her Facebook app

running and Hannah, frantic, used it to reach out for help. She
punched in keys.

Call911homehelp.

She hit the status update button a few times, fingers shaking
with sweat and blood, and waited, hoping someone would read it
and call for help. She was too scared to call and speak to someone
or keep the light on in case her dad was closing in on her. She
didn't know what he was going to do, but her upper arms stung
with his grip. Nausea rose in her throat and she gritted her teeth,
tears furiously falling down her face. She didn't dare breathe. Her
body curled into the corner of Noreen's dark closet, Zuzu beside
her, and she waited, praying to God for help.

⋮

15

The police left late that evening, and an ambulance sped to the hospital with Adam. He had suffered a complete breakdown and was thrown back into the memories of his trauma, induced by lack of medication and lack of sleep.

Hannah was a trigger, the family realized, piecing together the things he had shouted and his raging despair at his inability to save someone he thought was her.

Both girls went to bed in their mother's room after their night prayer. Dahlia was anxious to be at the hospital early in the morning so she and Hannah could spend the day there. Noreen had stayed up to pray at dawn and then immediately crashed.

In the middle of a fitful sleep, Noreen felt like she was falling off a cliff. Her body was shaking. In an instant, she woke up and realized her mom was leaning over her, prodding her gently.

"Oh my God, mom," Noreen gasped. Her heart was pounding and she still had a sense of vertigo from the dream-fall. "You scared me."

"Sweetheart," her mom whispered. "Hannah and I are headed to the hospital now. It's almost ten." There was light peering into the room despite Noreen having drawn the blinds and curtains closed.

"Mom, I can't move. I'm exhausted from cleaning last night."
"I know, honey. Marlene Auntie left a little while ago and she said you worked really hard. I didn't see a sign of the glass and blood we walked into."

At the mention of glass and blood, Noreen's stomach rolled.

"I just want to sleep for right now," she pleaded, not ready to face the world with a headache and the nightmare of last night.

Dahlia waited, mulling something in her mind. "I don't want you to be alone right now, Noreen. I really think we should go together. Your dad's probably not too alert right now, but I think it'd be helpful if we were all there for when he comes around."

A quick thought crossed her mind. If Hannah were in Noreen's position asking for some respite, would she be as pushy?

Noreen curled inside her blankets more, desperate to escape back into sleep. "Mom, I promise I'll be over as soon as I get up. I want to be there, too, but I just can't function right now."

Dahlia finally conceded. "Dr. Finland called earlier in the morning when he got into the psych ward. Dad's situation was as we suspected. He wasn't sleeping well and that was because he wasn't taking his medication. It's just a small setback, but we can see it as a reality check. I should have kept better track of his medicine."

"Mom," Noreen said, feeling just as guilty but uncomfortable her mom was putting the blame on herself. "We were all around. We all saw him. It wasn't something he announced he was doing. You shouldn't feel like it's your fault."

Her mom's tired face shifted into a little smile. "Thanks. I needed to hear that. This is just one phase of his progress. We'll get through it. I have hope."

Noreen murmured a response and closed her eyes, not agreeing or disagreeing, and drifted off again quickly. She felt the light touch of her mother's lips against her forehead before completely sinking into the welcoming abyss of sleep.

Noreen finally got out of bed in the afternoon. She stared at the ceiling, trying to digest everything that had happened. Her mind felt numb. The pajama pants and tank top she'd donned before crawling under the covers held the extra wrinkles of a fitful sleep. Glancing in the mirror, she looked in shock and disgust at her completely disheveled hair and the heavy bags beneath her eyes. Turning, she headed towards her closet only to pause and feel unnerved knowing that's where her sister had hidden from their dad, scared and injured.

A lump filled her throat, but she took a deep breath and tried to ignore it. From downstairs, she heard a door open.

"Noreen," a familiar voice rang out. "Sweetheart, it's just me, Marlene Auntie. I wanted to see you before heading to the airport. I picked up some green tea for you from your bakery."

"Coming," called out Noreen, grateful to leave the room. She walked quickly down the hallway and downstairs.

Noreen's nimble footsteps hurried downstairs. Marlene Auntie was at the kitchen counter they'd wiped down meticulously in the middle of the night. "I'll leave your mom's house keys here, Noreen," she said, hearing her approach while her back was still turned. She turned to face her, smiling. Noreen noticed her eyes widen slightly.

I must look horrendous, Noreen thought absentmindedly. *Oh, well.*

"Come here, you," Marlene Auntie held out her arms.

"Hey," Noreen said, closing in for a hug.

Marlene held her tightly, her tiny frame enclosed in a warm embrace.

"Oh, sweet pea, how are you doing?" She combed her hand over Noreen's hair, pushing wavy strands out of her face.

"I'm okay," Noreen said, forcing a smile. "Just sleepy. Trying to remember stuff that needs to get done. I didn't even brush yet so a little behind."

"You know," Marlene began, flipping back her own curly hair, "Sometimes it's okay to lose focus on those necessary things and just wallow. I know you're not the wallowing type, but have you given yourself a chance to just stop and be upset?"

Noreen scoffed. "That's Hannah's job. If Wallow was a kingdom, she would be queen of it for eternity."

"Mhm," Marlene responded, not planning on meddling in the sister hate. "You two do have different personalities."

"That's what mom told me, too." Noreen faced her with a rigid look on her face. "Mom really depends on me to be practical and keep things going."

"Maybe it's not so bad to remind people who love us that we're human, too."

Noreen paused, letting that comment sink in. Not sure how she felt about it, she decided to think it over later.

"When is your flight? Do you have to leave so soon?" Noreen asked, wishing she could stay a little longer.

Marlene smiled but was just as sad on the inside to be leaving, too. "I'll miss you girls so much. I've definitely missed your mom a lot. We should plan something around your giant family get-together and coordinate a girls trip."

Neither mentioned how a trip like that, with both girls and Dahlia, would only be possible if Adam got better.

"Let me get one last goodbye hug in and I'll let you get ready. Your mom said you'd head over after waking up. Your dad is fine," Marlene told her, looking directly into her eyes with a strong gaze. "He's stable and safe. You're all safe, too. That's the most important thing, Noreen."

Noreen nodded, averting her gaze. "I should go shower and get going." She wanted to leave the room before being pushed into more conversation about her dad. Today his condition weighed a lot heavier on her. Maybe because she wasn't distracting herself with school and things to do.

Marlene Auntie's words had also chiseled a little under the surface of her composure.

"Okay," Marlene sighed. "Call me anytime you need to. I can still lecture your mom, you know," she teased.

Noreen gave her a tight hug and they said their goodbyes. After Marlene left, Noreen showered and readied herself. Her jaw was stiff because she had been clenching her teeth, but she didn't factor that into the growing headache clawing against her temples.

She changed, prayed, and grabbed an organic oat and dried berry protein bar on the way out, the humid air grasping at her immediately. The storm hadn't left any remnants behind. Even the grass had dried into a brilliant green and was soaking up the sun. Noreen shielded her eyes as she drove to the hospital.

The elevator bell dinged and she rode it up to the psych floor.

Someone was rounding the corner quickly and Noreen ran straight into her as she exited the elevator.

"Sorry," exclaimed an unexpected voice. It was Felicia. "I didn't see you!"

"Oh," said Noreen, confused. She gave Felicia a once over. She had a few more piercings and some more of her usual heavy eye makeup.

"Are you here to see your dad again?" she asked Noreen. Her eyes, under all the makeup, looked tired and red.

Noreen nodded and assumed her eyes were similarly haunted from her own family's ordeal. "We had some stuff go on last night. Long story. So, here we are."

Felicia looked nervous and upset. Her hair hung limply and she seemed unsure on what to say. "Yeah," she finally mumbled. "It sucks."

"Is your brother okay?" Noreen asked, knowing he was in and out of the unit. Felicia nodded, looking uncomfortable.

"Okay," Noreen said, not interested in making further conversation since Felicia wasn't exactly Chatty Cathy today, "I'll see you later. My mom's waiting for me."

"Wait," Felicia implored. "How are you holding it together? Whenever I see you, you're like totally normal. I mean, it's just my brother who's going through issues but my life's falling apart."

Noreen fingered her necklace awkwarly. "I don't know," she admitted. "I guess I keep reminding myself that there's no point in everyone falling apart."

Felicia rolled her eyes.

Noreen felt flustered at the obvious rejection of how she managed to stay composed and on top of her feelings. "Well," she countered. "What are you doing to hold it together?"

"Anything to keep my mind off of things," Felicia grumbled, crossing her arms and revealing a hospital bracelet on her wrist. "And nothing works for too long. Even Keith tried to help."

A voice interrupted their conversation just as Noreen zeroed in on the bracelet and opened her mouth to ask about it.

"Noreen," called Hannah from down the hall. "We're in here!" Her head was wrapped in a purple scarf, sprinkled with miniature orchids. Hannah didn't seem as hesitant today, which was shocking knowing the ordeal she must have gone through the evening before.

When Noreen and Dahlia had reached the house in their separate cars, a few patrol cars were already outside. The storm was raging in full force, and some neighbors had come out under their umbrellas, shouting questions in concern.

The kitchen was covered in blood, and overturned fruit lay across the floor. Broken glass covered the breakfast bar from where Adam and Hannah must have struggled and knocked over a vase. Noreen's heart almost stopped when she saw the blood stains on her closet doorknob leading to where Hannah was hiding.

At that point, Adam was hurling things around the entire upstairs, furious and incoherent. He seemed like a madman, battling a nightmare only he could see. Dahlia entered with the officers and tried to help calm him. She couldn't maintain her composure as he fought with the police in her bedroom, swinging a picture frame into the wall. Finally, he was tackled into defeat.

Noreen turned and quickened her pace, walking into the hospital room with her mind a whirlwind of flashbacks from yesterday. Her suspicions were also growing about Felicia's actual condition.

Her dad was lying on the bed, asleep. Dahlia sat on the chair next to him. Her eyes were heavy with fatigue and stress, but she smiled at Noreen as she came in.

Hannah settled down into the armchair next to Adam.

"It took you awhile," Hannah commented. Her hand reached out to cover their dad's. Noreen was too taken aback by Hannah's movements to respond. She glanced at her mother in surprise.

Dahlia beamed at Noreen, who settled in next to her on a small hospital room sofa, wanting to share the joy of Hannah's behavior. She wasn't sullen and hiding in the corner as she would have been in the hospital before.

The previous night's traumatic events had caused Hannah to step out of her shell and see her dad's situation in a different light.

Not one to shy away from making things awkward for her sister, Noreen zeroed in. "How is it that you're so fine and dandy today, Hannah?"

Hannah barely looked back at her. "I realized that he's still there. Even though it doesn't seem like it, he's still the same person inside. He wasn't trying to hurt me last night. He really thought he was trying to save me. He must have been trying to save someone at the clinic, too."

"Noreen," their mother gave her a welcoming hug. "I know you just walked in, but could you pick up some dinner for us from the Tex-Mex restaurant by the freeway? Hannah and I haven't had a bite to eat all day and I'm sure you're famished, too. If you want to stay here, I can go," she offered. "It'll be better for us than cafeteria food."

It was almost surreal, to be speaking of normal things like dinner when their father had suffered a major breakdown. His breathing was steady and a machine blinked next to him. Noreen felt like she was living in an alternate reality, trying to keep up with facades and expectations.

"I'll go," Noreen said instinctively. "I'll pray here and leave. Time for *Maghrib* just kicked in." The pressure of being responsible and competent was weighing heavier and heavier on her shoulders. She wanted to be selfish, like Hannah, and indulge her own emotions, too.

"Thank you, sweetheart," Dahlia said, smiling. Noreen didn't feel any comfort in the smile. She hadn't broken down through the entire ordeal last night. None of them had tried to sleep before dawn; mother and daughters had spent the quiet predawn hour kneeling together in prayer with their heads bowed and hands lifted in supplication. Hannah had cried for hours after the police came and rescued her, refusing to go to the hospital for her own wounds.

Noreen's Facebook friends list was quite extensive. That worked in Hannah's favor. Several people commented with their concern and many, including Noreen's lab partner Leslie, had contacted the local authorities right away. She hoped it was a prank, but didn't want to take a chance in case there was a real emergency.

Marlene had also read the update after she finished her last session at the medical conference. Worried, she also phoned the authorities and rushed to the scene.

Thank goodness, Noreen thought. She didn't know if they could have handled him in his full rage on their own. Even with Dahlia and Marlene at the scene, extra and much stronger hands were needed to subdue him. As much as their mom didn't want him hospitalized again, she'd told them the road to recovery was going to come with several obstacles and hurdles to conquer.

Hannah had been patched up with a first aid kit, using the stinging alcohol wipes she hated. Dahlia's own eyes were red and swollen from crying and she constantly stopped to hold and hug her young daughter. The paramedics gave her a quick once over but Dahlia insisted that she would take care of her.

Noreen and Marlene Auntie busied themselves with the cleanup. Chatter was minimal. Hannah dozed off for a few minutes at a time as the night progressed, head in her mother's lap. Just before the sun broke the horizon, they prayed together.

"I'll call in the order from the parking lot," Noreen said, getting up to leave. "Marlene Auntie said to tell you goodbye. She dropped off your keys and left for the airport."

She kissed her mom on the cheek and then glanced at her dad, who was resting peacefully now, medicated and monitored. She spared Hannah a curious glance, unsure of what to make of her calmness after the drama she had endured. Hannah didn't catch Noreen's stare and was intently looking at their father with a new awakening on her face.

In the parking lot Noreen opened her phone. She felt unusually fidgety. Her messenger apps were lit with a number of messages. She opened Keith's first.

Keith: *Hey, game tonight, u promised 2 come!*

Noreen had forgotten, of course, in the middle of all the chaos. She didn't feel like attending a school game.

Noreen: *Sry, lots of stuff came up at home...see you at school*

She texted her reply and got into the car. After calling the restaurant and placing their order, she started driving, casually flipping through her phone and skimming texts at each red light. Keith's popped up again.

Keith: *Just stop by for a few – im sure u deserve a break*

Keith: *itz nice 2 get away sumtimz*

Keith: *plz?*

Keith: *Pretty plz with a scarf full of red cherries on top? ;-)*

Noreen shook her head. She was in no mood to go to a festive game, but maybe stepping in for a few minutes would freshen her up and take her mind off of everything. Against her gut instinct, she stopped at the last red light before the school and texted back.

Noreen: *Ok fine. But literally I'll stay for like 10min and go. I'm driving past the school now*

Keith replied in an instant.

Keith: *Meet u in front of stadium.*

Noreen pulled into the school and found some open parking spots far into the expansive lot. The place was jam packed. Students, many she recognized and even more she didn't, loitered in the parking lot and street beyond. She got out of her car and started walking towards the stadium. Cheers echoed from the crowded bleachers, open to the sky outside. She looked around and saw Keith standing several yards away. She waved and he grinned at her.

"Hey, thanks for making it," an exuberant Keith greeted her as she closed in on him. She was wearing a polka dotted shirt dress and black jeans. Her white scarf had faint silver lines in a meandering design all around it. Her huge accessory ring glittered under the stadium lights.

"No problem," Noreen replied. "I really can't stay long."

"Come on," he said, tugging at her arm. She pulled away so that they weren't walking so close and he chose not to comment.

She was still not sure why she agreed to come. After squeezing through dozens of people, they climbed the bleacher steps to where Keith was sitting with his friends.

His group nodded to Noreen and she sat down. They were passing around a huge container with a Coke logo on it. They watched the game for a few minutes and Keith began to joke around with his friends about the players. A couple of guys looked over at Noreen and nudged each other, smirking, looking at Keith with raised eyebrows. Keith furtively glanced at Noreen and when she wasn't looking, winked at his friends.

"Wait a second," Noreen mused. "If you're on the football team, why aren't you on the field playing?"

Keith chortled and his friends laughed uproariously.

"You didn't know Keith was put on probation for..."

Keith interrupted before his friend could finish. "Grades," he said. "My grades were awful last quarter, so I had to be benched."

His friends continued to snicker and Noreen glanced at her phone. Her mom texted asking if she'd gotten to the restaurant. "I should get going," she said, glancing at Keith and smiling in a half apology.

"You've barely seen anything," he exclaimed. The loudspeakers were blaring something, conversations were loud and frenzied, and it was all very hectic and bright. The entire stadium pulsed with enthusiasm and vibrancy that Noreen didn't have the energy to absorb.

"Sorry," she said, repeating her attempt to leave. She rose and stepped away from the seats, starting down the steps.

Keith asked her to wait. He took off his jacket and handed it to his friends, whispering something to one of them. The friend nodded and put the jacket on, reaching into the pockets.

Noreen was too distracted to notice the nuances of their behavior or to begin to suspect that maybe it was more than bad grades that had Keith on probation from the football team.

Keith hopped down a few steps to where Noreen stood waiting. "Can you help me find my car keys before you go?" he asked, eyes wide and hopeful. "I looked around before I came in, but I'm sure I dropped them where I was hanging out with these guys before the game."

Noreen sighed. She knew protesting would be pointless, so she agreed. He led her down the bleachers and out of the stadium, walking swiftly by a gate that was still closed. Her mind was still preoccupied, so she didn't realize their distance from the crowd. The uproar of the game was still very loud, echoing through the night. Noreen glanced around and wondered how on earth he'd be able to find anything in the dim light in this corner of the stadium.

"It was right...around...here," he murmured. "I think."

Noreen looked around the floor and didn't notice anything but light remnants of trash. Her phone vibrated in her messenger bag. "I don't think we'll be finding them now," she explained as nicely as she could, eager to leave and get on with her night. This detour to see the football game hadn't uplifted her as she'd hoped. "No offense, but it was pretty stupid to lose your keys. I'm sure you can get a ride home with someone though."

Keith smiled at her and came a few steps closer. His dimple wasn't as endearing in this sinister light. "You're real cute, you know that?" he asked in a lower tone.

Noreen raised her eyebrows and scoffed at the change in his voice. "Oh, okay," she choked out a laugh. "Thanks, but no, I'm not interested in being cute for you. I have to get going now." With those words, she turned, but Keith pulled her back by the wrist.

It wasn't gentle.

Her mind worked furiously. Keith must have misinterpreted something. She shook her head, trying to figure out how she was going to get away if he became physically insistent or aggressive. There wasn't anyone nearby enough for her to call, and with the noise from the game, no one would even hear her scream..

Idiot, she thought to herself.

"Keith, stop it. Seriously," she ordered him. He leaned over her, deliberately ignoring the command. There was a concrete pillar next to where he was standing, and in one maneuver he had her positioned against it and was pinning her there with his body. He groped his hand over her shirt as she struggled. Finally, getting tired of her attempts to shove him off, he pinned her arms to her side.

"Stop," she said louder, before he tried to close his mouth over hers. She reacted quickly, in fear, and butted her head hard against his face.

"Ow!" he shouted, letting go of one arm. She shoved the heel of her free hand into his nose and he stumbled back. "What the hell?" he yelled furiously, calling her some derogatory names. That sudden change in behavior made her freeze again. He backed away and she gauged the distance, figuring out where she could run and how long it would take her to get to safety.

Before she could move, a figure strode out and shoved Keith against the ground. "Get going," the person growled, lowering his face to Keith's.

Keith scrambled to back away, jumped up, and left the scene without looking back, holding his hand to his nose.

Noreen didn't want to stick around for questions. "Don't come close," she shouted. "My phone is on and the police are on their way," she bluffed.

"I don't think so," the figure surmised, slowly creeping closer into the shadowy, deserted area. Noreen's eyes widened slightly as her mind placed him.

"You're that guy from the wrestling team," she recognized aloud, her disdain clearly evident. "Is this what you school athletes do?" she asked furiously, enraged at both herself and the two boys she'd wound up with in the dark recesses of the stadium. "Corner girls and try to assault them in isolated places? What the hell is wrong with you disgusting perverts?"

He shook his head and raised both hands in a signal of peace. "Whoa. I only followed you two here because I knew he was up to something shady." The guy, with his ebony face, wiry body, and short, curly hair shrugged, looking at her. "Keith's been known to take advantage of girls. He thinks he's a charmer and always bets on...you know. I saw you two walk into this direction. If he tried to force himself on you, I didn't want the guilt on me for having walked away. Looks like you didn't need my help in fighting him off, though."

He paused, waiting for her to acknowledge his compliment.

She didn't acknowledge it.

"He's not allowed on the premises during games anyway because he was caught selling drugs months ago and his suspension was just lifted this quarter," he continued to explain, dropping his hands slowly. "I figured I'd leave you two to your business if you were buying off him, but you didn't seem like the buying type, either."

"No," she replied sarcastically, "I am not the buying type. Now, I need to *leave.*" Her voice rose at the end, emphasizing her desperate desire to get away from this fiasco.

Before he could respond, Noreen turned to stomp away. Suddenly, Keith reappeared with a few friends. They eyed their lone nemesis and looked ready to fight. Keith swore at Noreen as he got closer. "I knew you'd be trouble, more than that Felicia girl, but I'm not going to let you disrespect me and think you can just walk away," he threatened. "I'll teach you some manners you'll never forget."

The guy from the wrestling team stood taller, hands fisted at his sides. If there was going to be a fight, Noreen realized in dismay, her would-be savior was going to be pummeled. Feeling her gaze on him, he swiftly cast an eye on her and said under his breath, "Run through the passageway towards the inside of the stadium. The doors leading to the bleachers aren't locked. Get the hell away, NOW!"

As he shouted the last word, Keith and his friends attacked him and he started swinging back. Fists were flying, heads were colliding with cement, and she didn't think twice. Following his instructions, she flew into the roaring beast the stadium turned into at the end of a game.

She ran until she hit the series of double doors. She opened one, not looking back, and kept running. People looked at her curiously as they started getting up from their seats and streaming out. The crowd was still loud and uproarious. She felt safer in the middle of so many people and under more light. Looking around, she didn't notice Keith or anyone else following her. She struggled to get her phone out of her bag. Her keys were on top and she almost decided to leave everything and go back to the hospital.

Then she thought about the boy from the wrestling team and him not wanting the guilt of leaving her. She couldn't do that to him either. She dialed 9-1-1 and quickly gave their school name and the approximate area where she had been assaulted and where someone else was currently being attacked. The dispatcher assured her there were patrol cars on the campus and they were headed over there. Noreen was told to stay on the phone to give her name and more details of what had transpired. Until she heard sirens, she didn't realize she had a death grip on the phone and her knuckles were stark white.

.
.
.

16

Dahlia was livid and frantic. She strode into the police station and demanded to know where her daughter was. Noreen had called but had only said a few cryptic words about being at the police station because of trouble at a football game. She never mentioned going to a football game.

Her mind was reeling with Noreen's recklessness, and her anger grew at how senseless she could have been to get into trouble, especially now. Especially *at a football game*. Noreen didn't even like sports!

Frantically, Dahlia telephoned Marlene who had already decided to cancel her flight and return to the hospital.

In the middle of all of their family issues with Adam's illness, her usually dependable, reliable, and responsible daughter decided to flip the script. Now she was at the police station, nestled in the vintage building on Main Street. She tried to cool her temper before it boiled over.

It wasn't easy.

"Hello Dr. D," greeted one of the officers, sitting behind a desk under a small mountain of paperwork. The officer wasn't at all perturbed by the nervous energy emanating from her ob-gyn.

"Sylvia," Dahlia replied, recognizing her as one of her patients. She'd delivered her healthy baby girl just six months before. Dahlia remembered there was also a 3 year old daughter at home. Sylvia's face was curled into a tired smile, hair hanging down her back in a small ponytail.

"They put me on desk duty after my maternity leave was over. I have to wait for a patrol spot to open up and then I can really get back to the nitty gritty work," she explained. "Desk duty is pretty boring."

Dahlia didn't want to chit-chat. She wasn't going to be rude, though. "How are your girls doing, Sylvia? More importantly, how are you?" she questioned nicely, easing back into her ob-gyn shoes.

"Great and great," Sylvia replied. "I'm going to cut to the chase and lead you to your little girl inside, though. Don't worry, Dr. D., she didn't come in because she committed a crime or was an accomplice to anything illegal or dangerous. In fact, she phoned in letting us know there had been an assault and violent fight in a deserted corner of the stadium. We brought in a few other high school boys and they're going to keep me busy with all these reports."

Sylvia, or Officer Cooper as she was referred to at the station, led Dahlia down a small hallway. The police station was quaint rustic but warm. It was in direct contradiction to what she recalled from television and movies.

"I hope your husband is doing better, Doctor," Sylvia told her kindly before leaving her in the back area.

Four boys, bloodied and in handcuffs, sat on dark chairs, sporting swollen eyes and lips, disheveled clothes, and mutinous expressions. Officers were circulating among them, making phone calls, getting information, emptying pockets. A bag of what Dahlia recognized as marijuana was on the table next to them.

Dahlia's gaze narrowed in on Noreen. Her daughter was sitting against the far wall, not looking at anyone. Her eyes were fixed on the window above another corner desk. Dahlia was relieved. She didn't appear disheveled or hurt.

"Noreen!" called Dahlia.

Noreen looked up and heaved a sigh of relief. She took her messenger bag and walked swiftly to her mom. Dahlia gathered her in a quick hug, and then just as quickly shook her shoulders. "What on earth were you doing at a football game? You panicked me when you didn't answer your text messages."

Noreen's shoulders slumped. "I'm sorry," she started, her eyes heating up with tears she tried to blink away. Then she stopped and looked directly at her mom, eyes narrowing with more emotion. "I just had to get away from all the drama, Mom. I went to the game thinking it would clear my head."

"What?" asked a shocked Dahlia. "If you needed to clear your head, I'm here for you. You could have talked to me. If you wanted to talk to someone else we could have easily given you access to someone at the hospital who has more experience with…"

"No, Mom," interrupted a now very angry Noreen. "It's not that easy. I can't talk to you because you're on the verge of breaking down yourself. You won't admit it, but I can see that each day you're straining more and more to keep the pieces together. Hannah's already a hot mess every single day. I can't talk to anyone because I feel like I'm the only one who's holding it together. Everyone depends on me to be the one who's sensible and mature and never letting anyone down. Sometimes it would be great for me to break down, too. You're always trying to be so chipper that

I'm afraid of what will happen if you do give in and crack. I'm always providing that security for you to feel that we all can just get everything done and, well, you know what, Mom? Maybe you just can't. Maybe we can't. Maybe we're just all struggling too much to maintain a normal life with a crazy person in it and it's making us all insane. Did you even know that Hannah was getting teased and bullied at school for having a dad who's in the psych ward? Did you know everything I had to pile into my life so I could ignore what was going on at home? I haven't slept a full night in months. I can't stand that my dad came back from Syria as someone I can't recognize. I hate that I can't say hello to him at any given point in the day because maybe he won't recognize me. You can keep pretending all you want to, but I can't keep up with making sure you're strong enough to carry the weight of what our family used to be because it might never be that way again. The sooner we realize that, the better off we can all be instead of living a lie every day pretending we're all doing great!"

Her sudden and dramatic speech finished with a waterfall of sobbing tears. Dahlia was dumbfounded. Noreen had been internalizing everything from the second they heard of the attack on Adam's clinic. Maybe even before. Her pain had finally exploded inside, and Dahlia knew she had to help her pick up the pieces.

"Oh, Noreen. My darling," Dahlia whispered, holding Noreen tightly. They ignored everyone in the small lobby at the back of the police station. Noreen cried and cried. She finally stopped after several long minutes and started to apologize. Dahlia shut it down quickly.

"We have to stop apologizing for feeling what's very real," she explained. "I'm guilty. You're guilty. Hannah's also suffered a lot, and none of us are helping each other if we're becoming fragmented pieces of a whole, trying to pretend we're doing okay."

Noreen sniffled and nodded. "I love you, Mom," she said. "I don't want you to break down and go crazy, too."

Dahlia hugged her once more, compassionately. "I'll try my best not to let the crazy get to me," she tried to joke as Noreen sniffled into her shoulder. "Let's go," she said gently, using the loose ends of her cardigan to wipe her own tears.

They turned to walk towards the desk where more officers sat filling out paperwork. One nodded at them, politely ignoring their emotional scene. He was happy to see that mother and daughter were leaving arm-in-arm. Usually there were more threats and anger as parents and kids left the police station. He assured Noreen that she was free to go. "Thank you, young lady," he said, tipping his hat. "You could have walked away from a very dangerous situation, but we're grateful for your quick thinking and calling us. If we need to ask you any further questions, we will call. It may be that you will be asked to come into court, but we'll try to avoid that as you're still a minor and you've already given us a statement."

He turned to Dahlia and said, "Your daughter must make you proud, ma'am."

She agreed.

They were headed back into the hallway when someone shouted from behind, "Wait!"

Dahlia and Noreen turned. It was the boy from the wrestling team. His face was bruised and swollen, his clothes dirty, ripped, and stained with blood. Noreen felt terrible, but at the same time, grateful she'd had someone around who tried to help her.

"I wanted to say thank you," he said to Noreen. He looked at Dahlia and elaborated. "She could have just run away, gone home, and left me to get beaten up, but she was a real hero tonight. Thanks."

Noreen wanted to return his thanks for helping her first, but he sensed it and shook his head slightly, stopping her from revealing what had happened to her in front of her mom in case she wasn't ready.

The officer who had thanked Noreen stepped behind him. "Khalid," he said, addressing the tall, young man. "We are obviously not going to keep you because this was an attack. You can call home for a ride or one of our patrol officers will drop you off. Those guys," he motioned behind him, "will have a hefty bail because this isn't the first time they've been in here being written up. Their parents have been paying a mighty fine fee to keep their antics suppressed, but that's going to change quick because we're not letting them go anytime soon. This has been one time too many for this crew. Good luck to their parents."

The small group in the hallway said their goodbyes.

"Khalid, huh?" mused Dahlia.

Noreen looked at her suspiciously. "Khalid, huh, what?" she asked. She meticulously wiped the tearful residue from her face with a Kleenex she'd snatched off an officer's desk.

"Isn't it cute that you came to the rescue of someone who is named after a brilliant military commander?" Dahlia told her, teasing. "My little justice fighter. I think law school will suit you."

"Oh God, Mom," Noreen huffed, embarrassed, but also relieved that they weren't at odds. "The psych ward is exactly where you should be right now."

Noreen hugged her mom's arm close and they left the station, their joshing easing more of the tension both petite women carried on their shoulders. Noreen figured she could fill her mom in on the details of her assault after they had eaten and relaxed.

On the way back to the hospital, they stopped to get the dinner Noreen had originally set out to pick up. Even though it was very late, the popular Tex-Mex restaurant was still open and guests were spilling out into the warm night. They also stopped by their house to pick up clothes and toiletries. The hospital had ample facilities and provided decent cots for family members to stay overnight, and it seemed fitting that they spend the night together after so much upheaval.

Noreen remembered Felicia as they rode up the elevator to the psych ward. She hoped that she had escaped Keith's disgusting attempts at attacking her, too. She would try to find her tomorrow.

Mother and daughter walked down the hallway. Marlene had driven in not long after Dahlia left. She settled herself in position to watch over Hannah and keep a lookout for any rogue visitors who might awaken her. Her arms were crossed and head tilted, deep in conversation with someone. She had on comfortable jeans and a button-down top. Her wild hair was standing in all sorts of directions. She looked absolutely tickled by something the other person had said.

Upon closer inspection, Dahlia realized she was speaking with Daniel, or as he was known on hospital grounds, Dr. Manchester.

Marlene jumped up and engulfed Dahlia and Noreen in an enormous hug.

Dahlia's heart filled with warmth and love as she looked at Adam and Hannah. Noreen stepped in next to her and smiled, too. Her reservations and frustration about her baby sister were put aside, and she indulged in a feeling of love and peace. It was especially easy since Hannah wasn't aware of it.

Hannah had dozed, leaning her head at the foot of the hospital bed. Her hand, sparkling with the charm bracelet she never took off, reached alongside the bed and held her dad's. His eyes were still closed, but his face was more at peace than it had been since he had returned home.

⋮

5 Years Later

Dr. D!" called the translator in a delightful English accent. "Your next patient is ready."

Hannah turned, standing next to her mom outside the medical tent, soaking in a bit of the intense sun during her few minutes away from the steady stream of patients. This could be considered her lunch break, she surmised, tired but pleasantly motivated to go back inside and continue helping run errands for the small and dedicated team of medical professionals they'd arrived with three weeks ago.

"On our way," replied Dahlia. She finished the last few drops of lemonade from a paper cup and took it with her inside, lifting the white and blue flap to expose an interior of well-used folding tables and white lawn chairs. A few curtains separated the patients she and a midwife were seeing simultaneously. Hannah spent the mornings with her dad, who worked from another medical tent at the same refugee camp, supplying vaccinations to children. That required a lot of walking and talking with people through translators. Seeing a younger person amidst the injections made the kids feel less terrified. In the afternoons, Hannah came to her mom's tent and helped with anything she was directed to do.

Mona, her mom's nurse and eager translator, looked up from her clipboard, smiling as the duo entered the room. She and Hannah had become fast friends at the camp.

"This patient came in with her husband. I've checked her symptoms off on this chart and will have the lab sample processed soon." Mona's bright blue eyes flickered with excitement as she handed over notes for Dahlia to review. "They're quite giddy, hoping for some good news."

Placing her cup at the corner of a folding table to use later, she skimmed the information sheet Mona had filled out.

"How much longer until the test comes out?"

"Thirty seconds, Dr. D," Mona calculated, eager to see the results. "These are the moments I went to nursing school for," she continued, watching the second hand click closer to the half minute mark. "It took some grueling years, but I knew I wanted to make a difference for displaced people around the world. Finally, at the ripe age of twenty-two, I'm living my dream."

"Your parents must be very proud," Dahlia said in admiration of her determination. "Twenty-two is very young to be so certain about your life choices."

Hannah shook her head at Mona. "Now I'll be hearing it," she laughed. *"Look at Mona with her life figured out – get with the program,"* she'll say.

Mona grinned in response. "They worry," she admitted. "Mum and Dad never left England after settling in some 40 odd years ago. I grew up itching to explore and meet new people. Humanitarian work always appealed to me. It's heartbreaking but also rejuvenating. I can't imagine not being here." Mona's bright smile was contagious. Hannah grinned, too. It was lovely to gain personal insight on what drove people to refugee camps such as this, with their hearts full of compassion and love. "We have so many family members that were affected by the war," she continued. "Each has their own story and someone important who made their way into an uncertain future easier. Ever since the war started, I wanted to be one of those people."

The timer dinged. Mona put on her gloves and observed the results.

Even now, Hannah couldn't get used to what was being passed around in their small laboratory corner of the tent. Three weeks of writing down urine sample results, seeing blood drawn, organizing stitches and other medications for deeper wounds - it wasn't as gruesome as she'd thought it was during her first trip to a refugee camp, though she still wasn't completely used to it.

"Woohoo!"

Dahlia laughed at Mona's excitement and said, "Let's go and make their day." Dahlia lifted the flimsy cloth separating another corner of the tent and stepped into their makeshift patient room. As they finished up their visit, another three families walked in and spoke with the midwife, who was quick to start assessing their medical needs.

Today was the Jamal family's final shift at the refugee camp along the Macedonian border. Hannah and her parents had spent the past three weeks getting acclimated to the community of fleeing refugees who settled across the closed barriers. It had taken her less than 24 hours to feel completely at ease with the droves of people, especially children, who would regularly pass through the medical tents. The experience was humbling. Doctors, along with translators who had medical training like Mona, were in and out of the camps. Other people were there purely on a volunteer basis, offering their physical efforts to assist those who were seasoned and continuing their training on site a few times a week. Some only came for a week, others remained for months at a time.

The medical tent was situated at the edge of the camp, which was filled with thousands of smaller tents and makeshift canvas covered homes in which entire families resided. The war in Syria was nowhere near ending, and millions of people had courageously trekked away from their beloved homeland to find safety. There were even people in the camp who were fleeing from other countries in conflict.

So dangerous was their escape that many of those millions never made it to a safe shore, much less a refugee camp.

Dahlia and Mona congratulated the young woman as Hannah swept the dust that was settling onto the floor. There was always a small number of children who would wait for their own checkups with their parents. Hannah utilized the limited supplies available to keep them busy, making paper airplanes or holding puppet shows with characters made from old socks. There was definitely a language barrier, but they pushed through and found a small segment of delight during their day.

As she waved and smiled brightly at the children who had just come in, she saw the trepidation in their eyes. Quickly collecting a box of crayons and paper, Hannah sat on the floor next to them and held out her supplies. Excited, the children grabbed the crayons and papers and sat with Hannah.

"*Ahlan,*" Hannah said with her rudimentary Arabic skills. Welcome. "*Ismi Hannah.*"

"*Ismi Lubna,*" responded a girl, saying her name was Lubna. "*Ismuhu Hamza.*" She told Hannah the little boy next to her was Hamza.

As the kids took turns with their introductions and another midwife noted their parents' concerns, Hannah overheard her mom congratulate the patient and her husband after taking her vitals and explaining the care she would need as her pregnancy progressed. She wrapped up their time together by wishing them a better and brighter future.

It seemed to be a futile wish under the circumstances, but her mom always uttered the same words at the end of each patient's visit. She saw at least 50 patients a day, mainly expectant women who needed reassurance about their pregnancies and the occasional delivery. Younger children also frequented the tent for various ailments. Scraped knees, nursemaid's elbows, fevers, and even burns. The children who came made Dahlia ruminate to Hannah later about how their own lives were so vastly different. The lives of the children she saw daily had been different, too, not that long ago.

Several hours later, Hannah helped Dahlia finish up her shift and shared a tearful goodbye with Mona and the midwife from the Maldives, who was leaving the next week. A new team of doctors was going to be in the next day, and Mona would be their lead in showing them the ropes. There were several other medical tents alongside theirs, and once into a routine, the new medical staff and volunteers would work together to treat the growing refugee population.

"Hey," a deep and familiar voice greeted them, filling Hannah's heart with joy. "You two know we'll be back. Don't cry."

Hannah's dad hooked an arm through Hannah's and wrapped his other arm around Dahlia's shoulders. Mother and daughter wore soft plum colored scarves that tucked into their volunteer vests. Dahlia wore a white jacket over hers, with an emblem of the medical agency she was with. Adam's was the same. Hannah looked down at her khaki pants and beige shirt that were dusty from lifting boxes of medical supplies in and out of a truck and being on her knees with children.

"Dad!" Hannah greeted him happily. "How was the rest of your day? Did you get through the vaccinations?"

"All 300," he responded, squeezing her arm, happily. "Your arms must be sore from pushing those carts of syringes this morning. Tomorrow there should be a fresh shipment from the hospital for the new doctor who arrives to take over. As long as the kids remain healthy, their parents' worry will decrease tenfold."

"How true," Hannah's mom murmured.

"It's such a weird feeling. Going back home and leaving everyone behind."

"I know," Dahlia's eyes filled with tears again. I'll miss everyone here so much. Each girl, each woman, each mother and baby. All the doctors. Mona." Dahlia wiped her eyes on her sleeve. "I don't want to leave anyone."

"We'll come back," he told her. "As long as there's someone in need, we'll keep coming back."

She nodded, leaning into his hug. "Did you ever think you could come back to a situation like this after what you experienced?" she asked.

Hannah glanced at her dad as they walked, curious to hear his response. They were the same height and even strode in the same purposeful gait as they walked. "Yeah, Dad," Hannah prompted. "Did you think you'd be back at this end of the world, ever?"

Adam mused. After a few moments, he spoke. "I never thought I'd be back doing anything. There were some very low times after coming home. And if you three had given up on me, I might still be in those low places."

Hannah's heart squeezed with emotion. She remembered those low times as if they were yesterday, but also remembered the grueling, tiring, and emotional months that followed his breakdown. Within a year of medication, reflection, and the dreaded T-word, he was back to practicing and engaging in his relationships. It still took some time after that initial year to conquer his personal demons and make peace with the past, but he seemed to have done it.

She looked at the crowded and bustling refugee camp. The sun was slowly sinking toward the horizon. Eventually someone would begin to chant the call to prayer in a melodious tone. Most of the refugees were Muslim and many prayed together in congregation. Hannah joined when she could, since she had a less strenuous load than her parents. Other times she offered her daily prayers between tasks outside the medical tents.

She observed the life refugees were making for themselves. Borders were closed, government aid depleting, and hopelessness casting a shadow in everyone's eyes. There were tents as far as the eye could see, of course, but also sections where stalls of fruit and other food stood. People who had been driven from their homes were still trying to create a semblance of peace and everyday normalcy. Some tents were used as miniature schools in the daytime, while others housed men doing woodwork or women sewing clothes.

There was a poignant resilience in the pain of the refugees. A pain she ached to alleviate with what little help she could offer.

As they continued to walk toward the vans parked in waiting for the medical staff who would be departing for the night, Hannah took a deep breath of the balmy air.

"Hannah," Dahlia remembered. "Mona said she may be coming to the States to further her nursing studies sometime next year. The Texas Medical Center seemed really appealing to her."

"That's awesome," Hannah replied, excited with the possibility of seeing her friend back home. "Maybe we could room together if she starts next fall."

"That would be fantastic! Speaking of college, I can't wait to talk to Noreen. She wanted to video chat earlier. I hope she's not driving Marlene too crazy." She knew better, though. Marlene and Noreen had plotted their adventures months in advance.

Adam laughed. It was a robust and genuine sound that Hannah felt kindle energy and hope in the depths of her heart. Remembering the darker times made these brighter ones even more special.

"If anything," he said, "Marlene is driving her crazy."

"I know," Dahlia conceded, passing people who nodded at her and Adam and smiling back at them. Even after three straight weeks of seeing patients, there were so many new faces.

"Noreen said she finished her graduate school applications," Adam commented, angling Dahlia toward a falafel stand run by a boy who lived in the camp. "She sent some updates on WhatsApp and showed me a picture of her backup copies, organized alphabetically by university name and then placed in highlighted folders in shades ranging from yellow to red. Red being she wants to go there really bad and yellow being acceptable." He chuckled. "I hope the house isn't color coded when we get back."

"It won't be color coded, but I'm sure she'll have tossed all those spice boxes from the kitchen cabinet. Marlene mentioned they did some tidying up before leaving home for her grad school tour."

"She still has three more assault recovery talks to give with Felicia before they leave," Hannah put in. "A school in Dallas just invited them."

Hannah reminded her parents of her own plans for the coming months. "I'm so excited about spending time with Nana. Taking a gap year was definitely the best decision. It hasn't even been a full two months yet, but I already feel like I know myself better."

This was true on so many levels. Gradually, Hannah was evolving into a quiet spirit that sheltered softly brewing storms in her heart and soul.

"Don't remind us about becoming empty nesters, Hannah," her dad joked. He stopped their stroll in front of the rickety falafel stand and gestured to the young boy for three sandwiches. As the boy quickly wrapped up their food, her dad pulled some local currency from his pocket, exchanging it for the small meal.

It didn't escape her notice that he offered more than the price of the food. She hoped it helped the young entrepreneur and the family he was probably supporting.

"I think we'll find a way to stay busy," Dahlia responded, smiling and taking a bit of the fresh wrap. "And knowing our babies, they won't stay away for too long."

They continued walking and reached the vans, waiting for the remainder of their group to arrive. In silence, each observed their surroundings while they ate, soaking in the last few moments of their journey.

"Doctor!"

A girl shouted from a distance. People milled between the tents, most in a rush to get to their own tents before dusk settled.

"Doctor!"

"Do you think something's wrong?" Dahlia asked, squinting towards the voice. She couldn't get a good view and tried to stand on her toes to see better. Hannah had a better view with her height, but still couldn't ascertain where the voice was coming from.

"There she is," Hannah finally spotted her. "The medical tents are in the other direction but she seems to be headed this way. Maybe there's an emergency and she needs us to go with her." Not sure why her dad wasn't responding, Hannah looked at him and saw his face was frozen in shock.

"Oh, my God," he whispered. His half-eaten wrap fell from his hand. Almost as if he were possessed, he walked slowly towards the voice, eyes sharp and unwavering.

The girl yelling broke out into a run, speeding straight for Adam. The closer she got, the more Hannah felt she looked familiar. Perhaps she was a patient from the camp.

A split second later, the recognition hit home. Goosebumps crawled up Hannah's arms and her limbs froze in shock.

The girl looked exactly like her.

$$\vdots$$

Acknowledgements

Praise and glory for God, the Creator of the heavens and the earth.

A thank you to my parents, brothers, and children who facilitated avenues, knowingly or unknowingly—forcibly or willingly—for me to step into books and grow from the experiences held within.

Dutiful gratitude goes to the amazing sisterhood and support found in the spiritual connection of hearts. Named in no particular order of fondness: Roots, the Outsiders, Dysfunction Junction, Happy Hearts, La Sorellanza, Tahajjud CST, and Sacred Hajj Sisters.

For my southern saviors, my first friends in Spring. Your countless nights of help, warm gifts of sustenance, line by line analysis, and unfailing pride and support have floored me.

To the founder and executive director of Rabata, Tamara Gray: Thank you for helping us *#getwoke* for tahajjud and *#staywoke* for the barakah until sunrise. Thank you for highlighting the *#social-injustice* in our communities and telling us to get out and make a difference so we can spread some *#positiveculturalchange* instead of living a *#deafdumbandblind* cozy *#bubblelife*. Thank you for nudging us back into the *#aldente* groove from the wasted *#overcookedpasta* we had been conditioned to become through societal, cultural, and nafsi pressures. Thank you for the delicious #tearecipe that was sprinkled with #blessings instead of #bitterness. Thank you for not waiting until the #nomakeuprevolution became a trend to throw up your hands at the #commercialization of the #makeupindustry that kept us from feeling confident with ourselves - #barefaced and #naturallybeautiful. Thank you for the #voicenotes that rekindled the #joyjotsexperience for hundreds of women worldwide. Thank you for igniting the research on Star Wars #padawans in an effort to revive #spiritualawakening in the dimmest of hearts. Thank you for striving against the odds, staying strong for those who can't push back, and being firmly rooted in the legacy of the early believers. Thank you for your unbridled enthusiasm with each twist and turn in our lives and unfaltering hope that we'd not only survive, but thrive. Thank you for knitting together a #spiritualsisterhood that defies time and distance and gives us the ability to feel connected without ever meeting in person. Thank you for ensuring we find our happiness because we can plan for it - independent of forcing the #saviorcomplex on the people around us. Thank you for giving us ownership of time - an hour of learning, an hour of giving, minutes and timers and dhikr clickers that leave ripple effects of barakah in all aspects of our days and nights. Thank you for ensuring our toddler intentions get strapped to a leash, glued to a chair, and put into an enclosed trampoline so they may jump around but not wander off to find electrical sockets. Thank you for the Rabata #retreats and #daybreaknights. Thank you for being you.

⋮

About the Author

Afshan Malik is a Chicago native turned southern belle who was seen carrying briefcases of books across state lines during school vacations. After obtaining her undergraduate degree in English Language & Literature, she became enamored with the world of philanthropy and community organizations—pursuing her master's degree in nonprofit management. Her publications range from articles on parenting to the promotion of diverse authorship. Afshan continues to plot novels and life plans with the help of her charming husband and five delightful children.

Follow the shenanigans online at:

www.afshanmalik.com | facebook.com/afshanmalikwrites

instagram.com/afshanmalikwrites | twitter.com/afshan1009

⋮

Discussion Questions

1. What is the significance of the title, *Pieces*? Would you have given the book a different title? If yes, what would your title be?

2. What scene resonated most with you in a positive or negative way? Why?

3. Has anything ever happened to you similar to what happened in the book? How did you react to it differently?

4. Did any of the characters remind you of yourself or someone you know? How?

5. Were there any moments where you disagreed with the choices of any of the characters? What would you have done differently?

6. How have the characters changed by the end of the book?

7. What do you think will happen next to the main characters?

8. What are your reflections about mental illness and mental health after reading the story?

9. If you could sum up a main character in one word, who would you choose and what would the word be?

10. Is there someone you know in your community who may be struggling to cope with a loss, sickness, or other situation? How do you think you could help?

rabata
Daybreak Press

Daybreak Press is the publishing arm of Rabata, an international organization dedicated to promoting positive cultural change through creative educational experiences. Daybreak is committed to publishing female scholars, activists, and authors in the genres of poetry, fiction and non-fiction. It sponsors the Muslim Women's Literary Conference in October of each year and recognizes the fantastic achievements of Muslim women writers through the annual Daybreak Awards. For more information please visit us online at: *rabata.org/daybreakpress* or Email: *daybreakpress@rabata.org*.

⋮

Colophon

Pieces is typeset in Mrs Eaves, an elegant typeface first designed by the Slovak-born American typographer Zuzana Licko in 1996 for Émigré type foundry. It was styled after Baskerville, a transitional serif typeface designed in 1757 by John Baskerville in Birmingham, England. Mrs Eaves was named after Baskerville's live-in housekeeper, Sarah Eaves, whom he later married.

By studying books printed by Baskerville at the Bancroft Library in Berkeley, Zuzana Licko based her design on the printed samples, which were heavier and more aesthetically appealing because of the way the ink spread into the paper with the imprint of the lead type (rather than the original metal type). She reduced the contrast while retaining the overall openness and lightness of Baskerville to produce an elegant and a highly readable typeface.

Pieces was first printed in 2019 at IngramSpark US facilities and released worldwide. Printed on 50lb creme paper, perfect bound with a matte laminated cover.

⋮

www.ingramcontent.com/pod-product-compliance
Lightning Source LLC
Chambersburg PA
CBHW021018120726
47905CB00009B/3079